"Lex, I...I want you to leave," she said

She looked up and saw him staring at her.

"You don't mean that, Andrea." His face was anguished.

"Yes," she whispered, wanting to die. "I want you to go back to your daughter, make a new life and settle down—all the things you want to do." *All the things I wanted to be part of.*

"I don't understand," he said unevenly. "Why, Andrea, why?"

"Don't you see? You're not ready for another relationship." Her voice broke. "I love you, Lex, so very much, but it's not enough, is it?"

"You're wrong," he said. He was with her in seconds, his arms around her. "I love you, too," he groaned, "and I'm not leaving—not ever." Then he was kissing her, crushing her against him with a wild man's strength.

KAREN
VAN DER ZEE

waiting

Harlequin Books

TORONTO • NEW YORK • LOS ANGELES • LONDON
AMSTERDAM • PARIS • SYDNEY • HAMBURG
STOCKHOLM • ATHENS • TOKYO • MILAN

Harlequin Presents first edition November 1982
ISBN 0-373-10544-4

Original hardcover edition published in 1982
by Mills & Boon Limited

CHAPTER ONE

SOMETHING was burning.

Something was burning! Fire!

Keys poised in her hand, Andrea stood in front of her attic apartment, frozen. For interminable seconds she stared at the door, fear clutching her heart. Then slowly she looked down on her trembling hand holding the key. She didn't need the key; the door was open.

The door was open!

Nobody was supposed to be there. Sylvia was in Vienna. Somebody was in her apartment!

Andrea almost turned and ran down the four flights of stairs, back to the safety of the street. She hesitated, suddenly aware of the deadly silence inside her apartment. Carefully she pushed the door open a little farther.

'I don't like you living all alone in an attic in Amsterdam. The place is full of nuts and weirdos.' Her mother's voice, echoing in her memory. *'Why don't you come home?'*

'My home is here, Mama.'

'You're all by yourself. You'll be lonely.'

'Mama, I'll be lonely anywhere. I can't run away from it, don't you see? From now on I'll have to make it on my own.'

At least now there was Sylvia sharing her attic part of the year. It made her mother a little more comfortable, if not much.

Tentatively Andrea put a foot into the room,

silently pushing the door all the way open.

Nobody. Nothing. Silence. Only the terrible smell of something burning reached her senses. Was it food? It came from the kitchenette at the end of the room, separated only by a divider full of climbing plants.

Maybe her mother had been right. Maybe some maniac had found his way in and started a fire. Maybe he was hiding in one of the two minuscule bedrooms to the left. But there was no noise, no sign of life. Suddenly brave, she marched through the room, around the divider and into the kitchenette.

A smoking frying pan. A piece of meat charred beyond recognition. For a moment she didn't move. It was so incredible, she couldn't think or reason. Then automatically she turned off the gas under the pan and gazed at the meat. Who'd been in here? *Who?*

The sound of a door closing. Footsteps. Andrea whirled around, heart pounding against her ribs. A man entered the kitchen, looming large overhead, looking down at her without surprise. Black hair, bushy eyebrows, dark eyes.

'Andrea ten Cate?' he enquired.

She didn't know this man. She had never seen him in her life—she would have remembered. He was taller and darker than any man she knew, broad-shouldered, strong, frightening.

And he knew her name.

Sheer terror closed her throat. Wordlessly she stared at him, rooted to the floor. He had a long, thin loaf of French bread in his hand and he put it on the counter. His black eyes moved to the pan and the burned meat and something happened inside her. A cold rage overwhelmed her, sweeping away all fear.

'Who are you?' she cried furiously. 'What do you think you're doing in my apartment? Were you trying to burn the place down?' She was shaking with anger and she couldn't stop the words from coming out. 'Are you out of your mind? Frying meat and then leaving the place with the gas on full blast? Are you crazy? It's people like you who start fires! Stupid, careless, negligent idiots like you! People get *killed* in *fires*, don't you know? Babies and children and crippled old ladies and . . . and . . . fire-fighters!'

One step and he was in front of her, shaking her. 'My God,' he said in a low voice, 'calm down!' He pushed her out of the kitchen and into a chair. 'Aren't you overreacting a little? I burned a steak, not a building!'

Overreacting? How did he dare! What did he know about her? About what she had gone through because of somebody's negligence? What did he know of all the long, lonely nights. . . .

'Get out,' she whispered hotly. 'Get out!'

He didn't comply. Instead he strode back into the kitchen and returned with a glass of water. Andrea wanted to slap it out of his hand, but didn't get the opportunity. He made her drink the water, holding on to the glass himself, one hand firmly under her chin.

The glass empty, he put it on the coffee table, stepping back from her. She was aware of him watching her closely, but she refused to look at him. Instead she stared at her trembling hands in her lap. She felt suddenly drained and weak, with not an ounce of strength left in her—only the fear.

'I'm sorry I frightened you,' he said after a silence. 'I'm sorry I burned the steak. I'd just barely put it in the pan when I realised I had nothing else to go with it. So I turned off the gas, or so I thought, and went to the bakery across the street to get some bread.'

'The gas wasn't off.'

'I must have turned it the wrong way out of habit. My stove at home works exactly the opposite.' His voice was toneless.

Andrea looked up. His face was oddly expressionless. His hair was very dark and thick and much too long. His black eyes seemed empty.

'Who *are* you? What are you doing in my apartment?' Was he one of those 'nuts and weirdos' her mother worried about? He looked dangerous enough, with that black hair and those black eyes.

'My name is Alexander Vermeer, Lex for short. I'm Sylvia's cousin. She gave me her key and said she'd let you know I was coming, but obviously she didn't.'

'No, she didn't! She's out of the country.' Her voice shook.

Almost imperceptibly his mouth twitched. 'Don't worry, I've nothing evil in mind. Sylvia *is* my cousin. Her mother and my mother are sisters. Her father is a dentist. She has two younger brothers. They live in Apeldoorn. Sylvia studies Sociology at the University of Amsterdam and in the summers she works as a tour guide. Right now she's in Austria. Does that satisfy you?'

No, it didn't satisfy her. All his facts were correct, but she still had no idea what he was doing here, cooking a meal in her kitchen.

He was still standing, towering over her, looking down on her without much expression. There was something strange about his face, his eyes, and it unnerved her. The real fear had gone, but she felt far from comfortable.

'What are you doing here? Why did Sylvia give you the key?' She couldn't imagine why Sylvia had done that without telling her. Sylvia had shared her attic for the last year, and she was the most considerate room-mate anyone could have, bending backward not to intrude on Andrea's privacy, knowing how lucky she'd been to find a place to live in Amsterdam.

'I'm in the country for the month of August. I have to be in Amsterdam during the week, but not at the weekends. Sylvia offered me her room, since she's not here anyway.' He spoke in a flat monotone, as if he didn't care if she'd agree to the arrangement or not.

She didn't. She didn't want a stranger in her apartment. It was much too small and intimate a place to share with an unknown man.

A love nest, a friend had once called it—a long time ago. And for a short time, less than two years, it had been that—a love nest, hidden in the attic of an old house in the centre of Amsterdam.

He turned abruptly. 'I'll clean up the pan and then I'll go and have a meal out.' Andrea watched the broad back retreating behind the divider. She wanted to get rid of him, only she had no idea how. She couldn't physically throw him out, or keep him from entering again. He had a key.

Damn Sylvia! She got up from the chair and

walked into her bedroom. It was quite a pretentious name for the tiny space that barely held a single bed, a chair and a small wardrobe. Originally it had not been intended to be a bedroom, but when Sylvia had moved in, Andrea's father had come and partitioned it off. Sylvia now had the bedroom that Andrea had once shared with Bart. And now this man would be in that room. Closing her eyes, she sank down on the bed, hands clasped in her lap. I want him out, she thought. *I want him out!*

A short while later she heard him leave. She got up and went to the kitchen to fix herself dinner. Everything was in order, the pan cleaned and put away. She wasn't hungry, but she forced herself to eat a meatball and some fried potatoes. The first few months after Bart's death she had barely eaten, until she began to realise that she couldn't continue that way. She couldn't live for ever on a single fried egg or canned white beans in tomato sauce. She had started cooking herself proper meals, forced herself to go out with friends, signed up for an evening class in Spanish.

She had taken a deep mental breath. Okay, she'd said to herself, I'm a widow at twenty-one. A tragedy. I loved my husband, and now he's dead. I have to go on with my life. And I have to do it alone. I will have to get over this, one way or another.

She had started with slow, careful determination to wean herself from her past, from her memories. And now, three years later, she'd found herself a measure of contentment if not profound happiness. She had a good life, good friends, a good job. The memories were still there, but the bitter, lonely anguish had softened. Her tears were spent. She slept again at night.

She washed the dinner dishes and put them away, then made herself a pot of coffee. She watched the news on TV while she watered the plants. Lots of plants all around the place—a philodendron trailing along the slanted attic ceiling, ivy crawling up the trellis partition, a schefflera big as a small tree. In the corner next to the couch she had a papyrus plant sitting in a fish tank full of soggy soil.

Finished with both the news and the plants, she poured a cup of coffee and curled up on the couch with a book she'd just got from the library—*The Tamarind Seed* by Evelyn Anthony. She loved reading and soon she was totally absorbed, forgetting everything around her, forgetting the man and his intrusion in her life.

When she went to bed at eleven, he still hadn't returned. She felt restless and uneasy and couldn't sleep. It was almost midnight when she heard the key in the door, soft footsteps. The door to Sylvia's room creaked slightly. So he was back, damn him. A shiver went through her and she hugged the blankets closer around her. He frightened her, this dark gypsy of a man with his empty eyes and his toneless voice.

When she awoke at seven, he was already up—she could hear him move around. She searched for her robe, feeling irritable. Couldn't even walk around in her nightgown in her own place!

Passing the kitchen on the way to the bathroom, she saw him pouring water in the teapot. He looked up as she went by.

'*Goeiemorgen*,' he greeted her.

' '*Morgen*,' Andrea muttered in reply.

The bathroom smelled like soap and aftershave. A wet towel hung neatly over the rack. Beyond that there was no evidence that he had been there.

By the time she had dressed, made up her face and brushed back her hair into a ponytail it was seven-thirty. She didn't want to leave her room and face Lex. She added a little more mascara, a little more lipstick. Taking the clip from her hair, she swung it loose. She smiled wryly at her reflection in the mirror. Who was she fooling? All this effort for a man she didn't like, a man who'd barely looked at her.

He was a man who wouldn't look at her twice anyway. He was much too old, past thirty-five if her guess was any good. He'd think of her as nothing more than a little girl. But he knew nothing about her and it didn't matter. She knew who she was and what. And a little girl she certainly was not.

Memories came flooding back. Bart—his smile face, the love in his eyes.

'What do you think a man wants in a woman?' he'd asked her once. 'Nothing more than looks and sex appeal?' She'd been overly selfconscious about her body, her small breasts, her girlish face with that ridiculous upturned nose. But Bart had miraculously erased all such feeling of interiority, made her feel like a woman. He loved her, he wanted her, he made her feel special, gave her a confidence in herself she never thought she'd have. 'I love your smile, the warmth in your eyes, your unselfish heart, your generous loving in my bed. *Een juweel van een vrouw.'*

A jewel of a woman.

It was good to remember those words sometimes, even though they left her with a sad feeling of loss. It would always be that way.

She no longer felt any sense of inferiority or self-consciousness about her physical shortcomings, such as they were. She felt free and at ease with herself. If someone like Bart had loved her, someone smart and courageous and handsome like Bart, then some day someone else would love her again for what she was.

Someone else. . . . But falling in love was not that easy for her. She had no desire to settle for a medio-cre relationship with a mediocre man. She wanted everything or nothing.

She sighed and turned away from the mirror. It was time to have breakfast with the stranger.

He had set the table, a thorough job, too. There was bread and butter, cheese, jam, honey. The teapot was on the tea-light. He certainly had made himself at home, hadn't he?

Andrea sat down, feeling stiff with resentment and tension. 'There's a new roll of rusks in that green canister on the shelf behind you,' she said with barely restrained hostility.

He put the canister on the table. 'You like green,' he commented. 'Green curtains, green tablecloth, green couch. Like a damn forest.' There was the merest hint of amusement in his voice.

'If you don't like it,' she said coldly, 'you can find yourself a hotel. One thing Amsterdam is not short of is hotels.'

'And all full, in August.'

Andrea said nothing. She wasn't going to argue

with him. She wanted to ignore him, which was hard to do. She took a piece of bread, buttered it and cut a few slices of cheese.

'Tea?' he enquired.

'Yes, please.'

He poured the tea, and she watched him. If he made a comment about the green teapot, he would be sorry.

'Sugar?'

'Half a scoop.'

'You have a very nice place,' he said unexpectedly. 'When I was climbing up those god-forsaken stairs yesterday, I almost turned back.'

I wish you had. She kept her eyes on her plate and said nothing.

'I was expecting a student crash pad, but this looks very homey, very settled.'

'Thank you.' It was true. It was a cosy little place, but it had taken a lot of time and work to make that bare, empty attic into a liveable space. She remembered how ecstatic they'd been when they had finally found it. Bart had almost convinced her that what they should do was find a modern flat in the suburbs, in Osdorp maybe. But the clean orderliness of the new developments held no appeal for her. Everything there was too tidy, too planned, too organised, too complete. She found it deadly boring—no surprises there. She loved the old inner city, the ancient architecture, the cosy little bars and coffee shops tucked away in cellars below street level, the bridges over the canals, the boutiques, the antique shops, the whole atmosphere.

Bart had been good with his hands, building walls

and partitions, putting in bathroom and kitchen fixtures. They had scrounged around at auctions and the Waterlooplein flea-market searching for treasures to furnish their attic. They found a rattan chair, a crazy little carved coffee table, origin unknown, and an old farmer's cupboard covered with half a dozen layers of paint hiding beautiful oak.

They'd scraped and stripped and stained and painted. Bart had built a platform couch against the wall, with big drawers underneath for storage. Andrea had sewn the cushions, big overstuffed pillows in a gentle forest green. The whole place was decorated in various shades of green, the colour of trees and plants, restful, but cheerful just the same.

She took another piece of bread and spread jam on it this time. Childhood habits died hard. 'First a piece of bread with cheese, then one with something sweet.' She could still hear her mother saying it.

'More tea?'

She looked up. She resented him. She didn't want him here with his polite little questions and his courteous manner. He dominated the place with his presence, the bulk of his body dwarfing everything around him, making it all seem so small and insignificant.

He poured the tea without waiting for a reply.

'I realise,' he said slowly, unemotionally, 'that you don't want me here. I expect you'll hear from Sylvia soon. If her explanation doesn't suffice, I'll move out. In the meantime I'll try not to intrude on your privacy. I'll eat my meals out whenever convenient and I'll stay in my room.'

'Thank you.' Andrea gulped down her tea and

stood up, looking straight at him. 'I'm going to
work now. If you leave, please make sure the stove
is off. There's a baby on the floor below and
an old lady with a bad leg on the second floor.
They'd never get out.' She wasn't worried about
the young man living on the first floor. Being a
reporter he was gone on assignment weeks at a
time.

Lex Vermeer gazed at her silently, and Andrea
waited, eyes on his face. He made no reply. What
was going on in that dark head? She had never seen
anyone with such a total lack of emotional expression, such vacant eyes. Nothing she said seemed
to have the least impact on him. A profound sense of
unease settled inside her. What was the matter with
this man? Had he no emotions? No anger? No
laughter?

She turned and swung out of the room into the
dark gloom of the communal stairwell. A few
minutes later she emerged in the glorious sunlight of
a bright summer day. No tram today, she'd walk to
the office instead. On the corner the butcher's wife
balanced her enormous body on a stepladder as she
washed the shop window. She gave Andrea a cheerful good morning as she passed and Andrea found
herself smiling as she crossed the street and turned
the corner. To hell with Lex Vermeer. She wasn't
going to give him another thought, at least not
today.

Rush hour traffic was heavy and noisy—honking
cars, clanging trams, bell-ringing bicycles, growl-
ing mopeds and motorcycles. She crossed a bridge
across the Herengracht and turned right. At least
along the canal it was quieter, no room for trams
and buses. Many of the old town houses were now

used as offices for insurance companies, lawyers'
firms, export companies, and a variety of other busi-
nesses.

The office of Students Abroad, the organisation
for which she worked, was on the second floor of a
modest town house squeezed in between two more
impressive samples of seventeenth-century architecture, buildings with ornate gables and intricate
wrought iron railings along the steps leading up to
the heavy wooden front doors.

The office was quiet when she went in—she was
the first one to arrive.

Students Abroad was an international student
exchange organisation, whose head office was in
Washington, DC, in the United States. Andrea was
the assistant to Annette Raadsma, the woman in
charge of the Dutch branch of the organisation. It
was demanding and interesting work and varied
through the year. August was a relatively quiet
month. The old students had returned home, and
the new ones had arrived in June and July—twenty-
three in all, from nine different countries. They
would spend the year with a Dutch family and go to
school with other students. They would learn to
speak Dutch, ride bicycles to school, eat cheese for
breakfast.

Andrea smiled as she sat down at her desk. She'd
been a foreign exchange student herself when she
was eighteen, the year before her marriage to Bart.
She'd been sent to a small coastal town in northern
California, which had been nothing at all like she
had imagined. It was a town full of modest little
wooden houses and blue collar workers. There was
little wealth and a lot of unemployment. The scenery
and the beaches were beautiful, but the ocean was

cold. It rained a lot. It looked very different in-
deed from the images she had of California's sun-
drenched, palm-covered beaches, sprawling air-
conditioned mansions with large blue swimming
pools and tennis courts. All that, apparently, was
farther south.

The family she had lived with owned a nice, comfortable house without air-conditioning and without
a swimming pool. They had a colour TV, but it was
a small model. They owned a modest Chevette and
an old rattling Toyota pickup truck. Mr Swanson
managed a clothing store and Mrs Swanson was a
receptionist at a doctor's office. They didn't belong
to a country club; they did not play golf or tennis.
All of this was different from what she had imagined.
Living in America was not what she had expected it
to be, and it had been an interesting year, an educa-
tional experience.

There were noises on the stairs and the door
flew open. In came Annette, dragging a bicycle
through the door. Her face was flushed and her
reddish-blonde hair stood out in all directions.
She was in her late twenties and happily single, as
she described herself, having given up on men after
a disastrous love affair with a Frenchman. She
grinned at Andrea, raking a hasty hand through her
hair.

'Pardon my undignified entrance. I'll make re-
pairs as soon as I take care of this thing. I'm going
to put it out on the balcony. I'm taking no more
chances with those blasted thieves.'

Andrea didn't blame her. This was Annette's third
bike since April. But she was rather careless about
locking them up when she left them down in the
street, although she swore she'd chained her last bike

to a lamp-post the day it was stolen. 'They must
have had a hacksaw!' she'd said, but Andrea had
her doubts.

Having disposed of her bike, Annette came
back into the office. 'You're early. What's the
hurry?'

Andrea sighed as memories came back. 'There
was this man in my apartment last night,' she
began, and then stopped as she saw Annette's
expression.

'Don't tell me,' Annette groaned, 'you got scared
and ran away. Not a man has crossed your threshold
in years and you forgot how to handle it.'

Andrea couldn't help laughing. 'No, nothing of
the sort.' She began to tell Annette about Lex
Vermeer.

She left the office early and took a leisurely walk
home, stopping in the butchery to buy some ham for
the macaroni dish she planned on fixing for dinner.
There was no mail. Usually Ria, who lived on the
third floor, would take Andrea's mail up and put it
on the last flight of stairs, leading to the attic, but
there was nothing now. She heard the baby crying.
It always seemed to cry at the time she came home.
She felt sorry for Ria, who always looked tired and
unhappy. She was very young, married to a handsome blue-eyed woman-chaser who drank too much
and was never home.

The apartment was very quiet when she entered.
Was Lex home? His bedroom door was closed. It
was an eerie feeling not to know, but nothing would
have persuaded her to knock on the door and find
out.

As she put the ham down on the kitchen counter

she saw her mail. So he'd been out and had taken
her mail up on his return. There was nothing
interesting—the phone bill, the usual amount
of advertising leaflets, a card from a friend
vacationing in Italy. Andrea sighed. Nothing from
Sylvia.

She turned on the radio and began to prepare
dinner. The little kitchen was immaculate.
Apparently he had cleared the breakfast table and
washed the dishes. She boiled macaroni, fried onions,
mixed them together, adding tomato paste, cheese
and the cubed ham. Not very sophisticated cooking,
but she liked it. There was a lot of it, too, enough for
a couple of meals at least. Enough for Lex Vermeer
if he cared to join her. Only she wasn't going to ask
him. He'd said he'd stay out of her way and eat in
town, and he could just do that. She washed some
lettuce, cut up a tomato and a cold hard-boiled egg
and made a salad.

One plate, one fork, one knife. It was ridiculous.
It didn't make sense for him to go out and spend
money on a restaurant meal when here she had
dinner ready, hot and plentiful.

I don't even know if he's home, she thought. Well,
I can find out, can't I? Not a sound had come from
his room, but then she probably wouldn't have heard
with the radio on. She knocked on the door.

'Come on in.'

Andrea opened the door. He was lying stretched
out on top of the bed, arms under his head, staring
up at the ceiling. It unnerved her to find him that
way. What exactly she had expected, she wasn't sure.
She'd assumed he was here to work, but there were
no signs of any activity. No books or papers or file
folders, or whatever. Nothing.

'I made myself some macaroni,' she said, 'with ham and cheese,' she elaborated. 'If you want, you can eat here instead of going out.'

He turned his face and looked at her. Only it didn't seem as if he saw her. His dark eyes seemed vacant, his face devoid of expression.

'No, thank you,' he said, his voice without inflection.

She stared at him for a moment, but nothing more came. Softly she closed the door. Back in the kitchen, she sat alone at the tiny table and began to eat. Her fork trembled slightly in her hands, and she wondered why.

This man had the strangest effect on her, the way he talked, the way he looked at her. As if he were a machine without feeling, cold, unemotional, dead. What was the matter with him?

Somewhere in the depths of her being she was aware of a faint sense of recognition, as if somehow his manner and attitude seemed faintly familiar. She pushed the thought aside, picked up the salt shaker and sprinkled salt on her food.

Easy, easy, she admonished herself. Too much salt is bad for you. High blood pressure, hypertension, strokes, etcetera, etcetera. She sighed.

She washed the dishes and made coffee. She wasn't going to ask him if he wanted any. He was going to leave her alone; she'd better do the same.

Lex didn't emerge from his room all that evening. Andrea sat on the couch, reading her book, tight with tension. Was it him? The knowledge of him being in that room? Or was it the book? It was terribly exciting—the story of an English girl helping a Russian spy to defect to the West.

Spy. The word stuck in her mind. Maybe Lex

Vermeer was a spy, she thought suddenly, or some kind of secret agent hiding in her attic from God knew what. There certainly seemed to be an aura of mystery about him. Then she laughed at her own wild imagination. He was Sylvia's cousin.

Or so he said.

She knew nothing about him. He was a stranger. She felt profoundly uneasy about him staying in her attic. Still, she had to admit it was not a sense of physical fear. What exactly it was, she didn't know; all she knew for now was that she was going to bed, and that tomorrow she was going out with a friend to see a movie, thank God.

It was impossible not to think about him. Eyes wide open, Andrea lay in bed, listening for any sounds coming from his room. There was nothing but a thin partition separating their rooms, but for a long time she heard absolutely nothing. Had he fallen asleep? Or was he still lying there stretched out on the bed staring at the ceiling? He hadn't even had dinner. He hadn't come out of his room all night.

It was almost twelve when she finally heard him move around. For some reason, the sounds were reassuring. Soon after that she slept.

For the rest of the week she did not see him. Not at breakfast, not after she came home from work. But he was there in his room, she knew. As he had said, he was gone during the weekend, and she breathed a sigh of relief. Coming home from work on Monday, she sensed his presence as soon as she stepped inside. How she could tell she didn't know, because there was no physical sign of him, but she could feel it very clearly. God, she thought, it's like living with a ghost—a ghost in the attic.‟ I can't stand this.

She sank down on the couch. A pile of mail lay on the coffee table and she picked it up. Nothing from Sylvia. Damn her! What was she going to do? What was she going to do with that shadow of a man living under her roof?

She couldn't think of a thing. But she wasn't going to stay at home. She'd go downstairs and visit Ria, have a cup of her weak watery coffee, and listen to the sad tale of her disintegrating marriage. Talking to Ria always depressed her, but anything was better than staying home with the invisible man.

Sylvia's letter finally came on Tuesday, starting off with profuse excuses, which didn't do Andrea any good.

'By now you must have met that gorgeous hunk of a man, my cousin, Alexander the Great. (I do hope he got a haircut before he presented himself on your doorstep.) We didn't have much time to talk, and I'm not all that sure what he's doing in Amsterdam. Some kind of research, I think. He works for a United Nations health project in Bolivia. Anyway, he said he only needed a bed for a few weeks, and only during the week. I didn't think there'd be any problem, so I said he could have my room and I'd clear it with you. Well, I forgot and I didn't, and I'm sorry.

'I'm having a rotten time. I've never had a bus-load of people more cantankerous, complaining and dissatisfied than this bunch of oldies. Not one under fifty, I swear. And it's not usually the senior citizens that give me trouble. I don't know where they found this batch.'

Andrea couldn't help smiling. Poor Sylvia! Tour guide—such a glamorous job. Here she was in romantic Vienna, spending her time keeping grandmas and grandpas happy.

'One more thing,' Sylvia's letter went on, 'I told Lex to respect your privacy and to keep his hands off you, which is a big laugh, I guess. His mother told me he hasn't looked at another female since his wife died last year. (Actually not such a big laugh.) You should be safe, don't worry about anything, love, Sylvia.'

Don't worry about anything. Did Sylvia have no idea what she'd done? There was no way she could continue the way it was now. Andrea stood up. She was going to have a talk with him.

He told her to come in when she knocked on his door. He was sitting in a chair, reading. There were books on the bed and on the desk, heavy, big, serious-looking volumes bound in gloomy covers.

'I would like to talk to you for a few minutes, if it's convenient.'

'Go ahead.'

'I got a letter from Sylvia today.' She paused for effect, but he said nothing, just looked at her, his face a blank. Well, he knew, didn't he? He must have seen the letter when he brought up the mail.

'She affirmed your story. I don't think there's a need for you to find a hotel.'

He inclined his head very slightly. 'Thank you. I appreciate your hospitality.'

'Sylvia pays part of the rent. Even in the summer when she's away.' Fair was fair.

Andrea didn't know how to go on from there. She looked at him sitting in the chair, long legs stretched out, bare feet. He was wearing corduroy slacks and a green T-shirt. He still hadn't had a haircut, and he didn't look at all like the stereotype image she had of a United Nations employee, but preconceived stereotypes were very deceiving—she had learned that when she'd gone to live in California.

'There's no need for you to hide in your room to the extent that you have,' she said.

His eyebrows quirked up. 'Hide?'

'Today is the first time I've seen you in a week.'

'I was informed that you like your privacy.'

'I do. But I don't mind saying hello and goodbye on occasion, or sharing a meal once in a while. This is a very small place, and I know you're here in this room. If I never see you it feels as if I'm living with a ghost.'

His lips twitched in a shadow of a smile. Good heavens, he was smiling, he really was.

'You are very straightforward, aren't you? And very sure of yourself,' he commented mildly.

Andrea ventured a smile. 'I try my best.'

It was easier after that. They saw each other at breakfast and dinner, but that was about all. They had innocuous little conversations, about the weather, the food they were eating, the crowded beaches, the housing shortage in the cities. By unspoken agreement they stayed away from the personal and the private. After two weeks of this Andrea still knew nothing about him.

Nothing except one thing.

CHAPTER TWO

His apparent unemotional behaviour, his total lack of interest in everything around him, hid a numbing grief. He was like a man without a purpose, without a will to live. He was a shell with empty eyes, with a heart that felt not even loneliness.

And in him Andrea recognised herself—the person she had once been, three years ago.

The knowledge about him altered her feelings for him. Strange things happened in her mind. She wondered what he would be like as a happy man—a man with a smile in his eyes and laughter in his voice. Her fear of him had disappeared, had been replaced by fascination mixed with a measure of compassion. She began to think about his wife. She knew nothing about her, not even her name, or if she was Dutch. Lex could have married a dark-haired Bolivian beauty, after all. She started imagining him as a loving husband, kissing his wife, smiling, tender. He was a strong, rugged sort of man, but she sensed in him a gentleness. Why, she could not say. She wondered how it would feel to be held in his arms, to be kissed by him.

So, she thought wryly, it has come to this.

He surprised her one day by inviting her to dinner.

'I appreciate your hospitality,' he said. 'So—no cooking for you tonight. We'll go to the Leidseplein and find a nice place to eat.'

For a moment Andrea was too surprised to speak.

He was smiling at her, a faint smile, but it was such a change. When she didn't answer immediately he raised his eyebrows in question.

'Don't you want to?'

'Oh, yes, I'd love to!'

It was different, somehow, being with him in a restaurant, away from the intimate confines of her attic. Conversation was easier, a little more relaxed and less inane. The wine helped, no doubt. Lex had taken her to La Belle Epoque, next to the theatre, and it was like being in a different world, the unique decor of the restaurant creating its own special atmosphere. The food was delicious and she enjoyed being here with Lex, seeing him unwind a little.

She ventured to ask about his work in Bolivia, and saw him frown. She hoped fervently she hadn't asked the wrong question and spoiled his good mood.

'It's not a very inspiring story,' he replied after a moment's hesitation.

'No? I'm sorry. . . .' She was angry with herself for having asked. 'I was just wondering. I don't know anything about Bolivia, but if you. . . .'

'Bolivia is many things,' he said obscurely. 'It's beautiful and fascinating and distressing, depending on where you are and what you do.' He twisted the stem of his glass and examined the swirling wine. There was a long pause. Then he began to speak, slowly at first, not looking at her.

He was a doctor, heading the medical team of a comprehensive medical and nutrition project aimed at bringing some sort of organised health care to the rural Indians. Their living conditions were abominable. He had been many places, seen much that didn't please the eye or the heart, but never anything like this. There was extreme poverty, hunger and illness, not to mention illiteracy and lack of formal education. The climate was hostile, the altitude too high for health and comfort, the soil dry and barren.

He raised his head, his glance meeting hers. 'In the area where we work,' he said slowly, 'the life expectancy is thirty-five years. Sixty per cent of the people have tuberculosis, and more than half the children die before they're five years old.' He spoke the words quietly, carefully as if to make sure they lost none of their meaning.

They didn't. Andrea was appalled. 'It's horrible,' she said, her voice low. Her words were totally inadequate, but was there anything meaningful to say about an account of so much suffering? She looked down on the food on her plate, feeling an acute sense of guilt. Raising her head, she met his eyes.

'Enjoy it,' Lex said softly, as if he knew exactly how she felt. 'Be grateful you're one of the lucky ones.'

She was silent. One of the lucky ones. Yes, in so many ways she certainly was that.

'Have some more wine.' He picked up the bottle and filled her glass. 'It wasn't my intention to depress you. Why don't you tell me about your work?'

Eager for a change of subject, she began. There was plenty she could tell him about her job, and he seemed amused when she told him some of the stories about the foreign students she dealt with. He smiled and shook his head as she recounted the story of the American girl who'd arrived in Amsterdam with ten big jars of peanut butter because she'd thought it to be an unknown commodity in Holland and she'd been convinced she couldn't survive an entire year without.

It made her happy to see him smile, to see the amusement in his eyes. They softened the hard lines of his face, made him seem less alien and distant—if only for a moment. But in that moment Andrea caught a glimpse of a man who had once been happy and whole, and a longing welled up in her to know him that way. She wondered what it would take to break down the dark walls he had built up around himself, to make him happy again.

The meal was finished and they were sipping the last of the wine, when unexpectedly he took her hand and glanced down at her fingers.

'No ring,' he commented. 'Or rings.'

His touch went like a shock wave all the way through her and her heart lurched. She sat very still. 'No.'

No ring, no rings. After Bart's death she had taken his wedding band and worn it next to her own, marking her to the world as a widow. But she had been only twenty-one and she could not bear people's pity, or their amazement. She could not spend her life as the poor young widow, so she had taken the rings and put them away. It was not a rejection of Bart's love, or their marriage. That would forever be part of her and her memories, but it was none of the world's business.

Lex was still holding her hand. In the dark eyes she saw a flicker of interest, the first genuine interest in her as a person.

'Andrea ten Cate, *Mrs* ten Cate,' he said quietly. 'I saw it on your mail.'

'My husband died. Three years ago.'

'My God! How old were you?'

'Twenty-one.'

He looked at her intently, silently. She knew he wouldn't ask.

'He was a firefighter,' she said. 'He died in a fire trying to rescue a mother and her newborn baby.' She could talk about it now without going all to pieces. She had dealt with her grief and learned to accept it.

And what about you? she asked silently. *What about your wife? How did she die?* But she could not—dared not ask that question out loud.

'I see,' he said softly. 'Now I understand.'

'Understand what?'

He gave a crooked little smile. 'Your reaction to my burning the steak my first night here.'

For the rest of her life, fires and anything connected with them would hold a sense of terror for her. She had become meticulous about turning off the gas, checking ash trays if she'd had company, replacing worn electrical cords—anything. Every time she heard the heart-chilling whine of a fire truck she'd break out in a cold sweat.

Gently Lex released her fingers. There were no more questions, and she asked none of her own. He would have to volunteer to talk about himself, or to give her some indication that he would welcome her interest. Up to now he had been so tight, so close, so totally uncommunicative that certainly he wouldn't drop the barrier just in one pleasant evening.

On Monday Andrea came home soaked by a summer rain, finding a pot of tea steeping on the tea-light. It was lovely to come home that way. It reminded her of her schooldays when her mother would wait for her to come back from school, tea and cookies ready on the table. There was nothing more welcoming on a cold or wet day.

Quickly she changed into dry clothes, jeans and a shirt, and brushed out her wet hair. It needed a trim. Her bangs were getting too long, hanging almost in her eyes. Maybe she should have a colour rinse this time, or maybe she should go for blonde. Blondes had more fun, or so they said. Brown hair was so dull, so ordinary.

'You're so ordinary!' She smiled as she remembered the words spoken by the ten-year-old girl in her American family in California. *'I didn't think you'd look like that!'*

Little Cassy had expected braids and wooden shoes and lacy caps and heaven knew what else. Wasn't that what Dutch girls wore? She had been very disappointed. Andrea looked like thousands of American girls—blue eyes, brown hair, long and straight and swinging loose around the shoulders. Andrea grimaced at her reflection. Ordinary—like thousands of Swedish girls and German girls and English girls as well.

She poured the tea, then knocked on Lex's door, calling his name, asking whether he wanted it in his room or in the living room. He opened the door and stepped out.

'I'll have it out here, if you don't mind. I need a break.'

He looked terrible—miserable, grey—worse than she'd seen him in the last few weeks. Concern tugged at her heart. She carried the tray to the living room and put it on the table, then sat down and gazed at him as he seated himself in the rattan chair, which creaked in protest under his weight. He stared off into space, drinking his tea without saying a word.

'Aren't you feeling well?' Andrea asked after a silence.

His eyes moved to her face and he looked at her blankly, as if he didn't understand her question. 'I'm fine,' he said at last. 'Just fine.'

Again the minutes passed in silence.

'I was thinking of cooking Nasi Goreng for dinner,' she said in an attempt to fill the silence with words. 'Do you like Indonesian food?'

'Yes, I do. That would be nice.' He spoke politely, absently, not really looking at her. His expression worried her.

'My husband liked Indonesian food,' she continued. 'We'd often go out to one of those little restaurants near the Dam.' She didn't know what made her say that, to volunteer this information to him. As if somehow she wanted to make him understand that it was possible for her to talk about Bart now. That one day it would be possible for him to talk about his wife.

I know how it hurts, she wanted to say. I know how terribly hard it is.

But Lex made no comment. He stared blindly into his cup, his thoughts far away. She knew she could not reach him—not yet, maybe never.

He said nothing at all during dinner, shovelling in his food without tasting it, or so it seemed. Andrea had never seen him so tense—the muscles of his face and neck hard and taut, his movements jerky. What had happened over the weekend to make him like this? Where had he gone in the first place? To his parents? So many questions and no answers.

She stood up to clear the table and she was next to him reaching for his plate. But instead of taking it she touched his arm, very gently, almost involuntarily.

'Would you like me to give you a massage?'

He stared at her without speaking, and suddenly she was sorry she'd made the suggestion. Massage was a terribly intimate activity, at least for her it had always been. How had she got it in her head to suggest such a thing to him?

'A body massage?' Lex asked after a few interminable moments.

She swallowed nervously. 'Yes.'

'Do you know how?'

She nodded. 'My sister taught me. She's a medical masseuse.'

She taught me so I could help Bart, she added silently. Every time he'd come home from one of those horrible fires he was strung so tight he couldn't relax. We'd spread out a folded sleeping bag on the floor and he'd lie down with his clothes off and I'd give him a massage, starting with his face and working my way down to his feet. It was the only way he could ever relax. Sometimes he'd fall asleep right there on the floor, and sometimes he'd pull me close and we'd make love. . . .

And suddenly, as all those unspoken words went through her mind, she caught his eyes on her and blood rushed into her cheeks. A slow smile softened his features.

'Ah, you surprise me, Andrea. You surprise me very much, standing there blushing like a virgin. I wonder why.'

Quickly she took his plate and turned her back on him. What was he thinking? Oh, God!

With an effort she regained her composure. 'Would you like yoghurt for dessert? Or just coffee after I've done the dishes?' Her voice, miraculously, was calm.

'I'd like a massage.'

'I'm sorry I suggested it. It was a stupid thing to do. Obviously you got the wrong idea.'

'No, I didn't.'

She still stood with her back turned to him, rinsing the dishes. She did not reply.

'You're a very generous person, Andrea. A massage would help—I know I'm wound tighter than a coil.' He paused for a moment. 'You don't strike me as hopelessly desperate.'

Desperate? Desperate for love, desperate for a man's touch? No, not *that* desperate! The water was streaming over her idle fingers. Lex wasn't exactly desperate himself, either, was he?

She heard his chair move and then he was standing next to her—very close. She was very aware of his nearness and she stared at the plate in her hand, silent and tense.

'You're not saying anything,' he said softly. 'You're a quiet kind of person, aren't you?'

She looked up, meeting his eyes. 'So are you.'

For a moment longer he held her eyes, then he reached for the dishbrush. 'I'll wash, you dry,' he said.

They took care of the dishes in total silence. His thoughts were far away again, she could tell. If only he would talk. But why would he talk to her? He didn't know her. They were strangers, total strangers sharing a converted attic for a few short weeks.

Lex took his coffee with him into his room, saying he had work to do. He had told her he was doing research, something to do with nutrition and the treatment of tuberculosis. More than half the Indians in the area where he worked suffered from the disease, a number that had staggered her.

She found a magazine, last week's *Libelle*, and tried to read, but not even Sheherazade's warm and witty column could hold her attention. Lex was on her mind. He had not mentioned the massage again and she knew he was no longer expecting it. She thought of the anguish in his dark eyes, the tenseness of his body. What was he doing right now? Was he really working, or just lying on his bed, staring up at the ceiling in rigid immobility?

She got up abruptly and threw the magazine down. She watered the plants, dusted the bookshelves, cleaned out the kitchen junk drawer. Incredible what all didn't end up in there—a sample tube of baby cream, an old postcard from Sylvia, a man's cufflink, some French coins, half a roll of King peppermints and a package of chewing tobacco. *Chewing tobacco*, for Pete's sake! Andrea examined it for a moment before tossing it in the waste basket. It was old and dried out. She had no idea where it had come from. One of Sylvia's friends, was her best guess.

It was almost ten o'clock. Not a sound from Lex's room. His face flashed before her eyes and with a deep mental breath she went to the living room, opened the drawer under the couch and took out the sleeping bag. Having moved the chair and the coffee table aside, she spread it out on the floor and covered it with a sheet.

She moved around automatically, trying hard to

ignore her increasing nervousness. Searching through her records, she selected a few and put them on the stereo turntable. In the kitchen she poured some oil into a plastic dispenser bottle and put it in a pan of warm water. Corn oil would have to do.

There were noises coming from Lex's room now and she was about to knock when his door opened. He stood in front of her, toilet bag in hand, towering over her. Her heart beating frantically, she looked up at him.

'I'll give you that massage, if you're still interested.'

His dark eyes held hers without smiling. 'I would like that very much. I didn't mean to make you feel uncomfortable.'

'It doesn't matter.'

'I was just going to take a shower. I won't be long.'

She stepped aside and he passed her, going into the bathroom. When he came out a while later he had a large towel wrapped around his waist.

'What would you like me to wear? Is this all right or shall I put on some jeans?' There was not the slightest hint of mockery in his voice.

With her heart thudding wildly in her chest, Andrea looked at the dark, muscled torso. 'The towel is fine,' she managed. She couldn't give him much of a massage with half his body wrapped up in denim.

I must be crazy! she thought in icy panic. I can't come close to him, touch him! But another part of her was laughing, mocking. You've seen a man without clothes on before, haven't you? You were married once, remember? What's so different about this? What's there to get nervous about?

She didn't know the what or the why, and it didn't matter any more, it was too late now. What she had to do now was stay calm and not act like a fool.

Lex moved over to the sleeping bag and lay down, eyes closed. His arms were stretched out next to him, his hands clenched. 'Would you mind turning off that big light?' he asked.

'No. I was going to.' She flipped the switch and knelt down by his side and took his hand, gently opening his fingers. 'Try to relax. I'll put on some music—that may make it easier.' She came to her feet and turned the stereo on, and soft piano music flowed through the room, relaxing, but otherwise quite innocuous.

'Nice,' he said. 'Very nice.'

She knelt down behind his head and rubbed a little warm oil on her hands. She centred her palms on his forehead, fingers extended down to the temples. With all her might she tried to be calm and detached, but her heart refused to go back to its normal rhythm.

Just give the man a massage, she told herself irritably. He's got a body like anybody else, with a head and arms and legs and groups of muscles. Just concentrate on what you're doing and forget the rest.

What rest?

She closed her eyes for a moment. Then she took in a slow deep breath.

'I want you to concentrate on your breathing,' she said, explaining what she wanted him to do. 'By the way, do you wear contact lenses? You'll have to take them out.'

A faint smile. 'No.'

She began to massage his forehead, starting in the

centre with her thumbs, moving them in both directions down to the temples. She did his forehead, his
eyes, his cheeks, his chin, feeling all the time the
tightness of his muscles, willing them to relax under
her touch.

'Don't clench your jaws,' she admonished gently.
'Try to relax those muscles.' She kept moving her
thumbs in slow circling motions until finally she felt
the tightness ease off.

'God, that feels good,' he murmured.

The room was pleasantly dim, with only one small
light on near the couch. The music flowed softly
around them, but it failed to soothe her nerves.
Seeing and touching this almost naked male body in
front of her on the floor was an unnerving experience, bringing thoughts to mind she didn't want to
linger on.

She examined him critically as she worked, trying
to find fault with the big, muscular physique, as if
somehow that would make it easier. Well, he wasn't
perfect, she concluded with ridiculous satisfaction.
His chin was too hard and square, and his nose could
have been a little less prominent. For the rest he
seemed quite perfectly proportioned, although
maybe his feet needn't have been quite so large. A
very nice specimen, she told herself analytically, surveying the broad shoulders and chest, the narrow
hips, the straight legs.

He lay very still, his eyes closed. She massaged his
neck and shoulders, his arms and chest, and after a
while she could feel the tension flow out of him. It
was hard work and her hands began to ache. She
hadn't done this for quite some time. After she had
massaged his legs and feet, she asked him to turn
over so she could do his back.

'I don't want to move,' he murmured. 'Forget my back.'

She was sitting on her knees by his side, looking at him lying there half asleep and peaceful, and it made her happy.

Slowly Lex half-opened his eyes. 'Maybe I'll just go to sleep right here. Would you mind?'

She smiled and shook her head. '.Nee. I'll get you a sheet and blanket, or you'll get cold.'

He reached out and took her hand, rubbing her fingers gently. 'Miracle hands,' he murmured, his eyes closing again. 'What's that stuff you were using on me?'

'Salad oil. Corn oil, to be exact. It was the best I could do at such short notice.'

He groaned. 'I must be as slithery as an eel!'

'Good for your skin,' she commented lightly.

He opened his eyes again and gently tugged at her hand. 'Come here,' he said softly, holding her eyes as she moved closer. And then his other arm came up and he pulled her on to his chest, her face against his. He kissed the corner of her mouth, then moved his lips to cover hers. Her heart hammered wildly against her ribs, the blood thundered in her ears.

'Thank you,' he murmured against her lips. 'Thank you, sweet Andrea. I haven't felt like this for a very long time.' He kissed her again—softly, gently. Then he released her, smiling at her, his eyes closing again. There was no resistance as she moved away from him.

She had done her job very well—he was sound asleep.

A soft sound woke her the next morning. Opening

her eyes, she found Lex next to her bed, a cup of tea
in his hand. Incredulous, she stared at him, and he
gave a faint smile, obviously amused by her expression.

'*Kopje thee?*'

'Mmm . . . tea in bed. What luxury!' She sat up,
putting the pillow behind her back and pulling the
blankets under her arms. Not that it was necessary.
Her cotton-knit night shirt was quite unrevealing,
designed for comfort rather than seduction. She took
the cup from him.

'*Dankjewel*. I feel spoiled.'

'It's the least I could do. Last night I slept as
I haven't slept for a very long time, thanks to
you.'

Andrea sipped the tea. It was hot and strong, the
way she liked it. 'Did you stay on the floor all
night?'

He shook his head. 'I woke up a couple of hours
later and staggered off to my bed and went right
back to sleep.' He moved to the door. 'I'll get breakfast ready. Would you like a soft-boiled egg?'

'Yes, lovely. Thank you for the tea.'

At some point during breakfast she became aware
of him watching her. Looking up from her plate, she
saw an expression of curious contemplation in his
eyes.

'Why are you looking at me like that?'

'I'm wondering why you never ask me any questions.'

'Because you don't want me to.' She was very sure
about that. There was a wall of reserve around him
with warning signs all over it.

'Don't you want to?'

'Of course I want to,' she answered quietly. 'You

live under my roof and I know almost nothing about you. It seems strange sometimes.'

'Hasn't Sylvia told you anything?'

'In her letter she wrote that you live in Bolivia and work for the U.N., and that you lost your wife last year.' There was no change in his expression as she spoke the words. She took another swallow of tea. 'That's all I know.'

'I see.' He stared in his cup, making no further comment.

When they had finished eating, Andrea stood up and began to clear the table. Lex helped her, putting away the cheese and honey.

'Would you like to go to a movie tonight?' he asked.

She turned to look at him. 'There's no charge for my service,' she said lightly, smiling a little.

He gave her a long look. 'I didn't think so. And that's not what I meant. I'd like to go out and have a little diversion, and I'd like it if you'd come with me.'

'In that case, yes, please, I'd like that.'

A faint smile. 'Good.'

They saw a French movie, a wildly humorous tale of the misadventures of a couple taking a trip from Paris to Hong Kong in a converted bus. Andrea hadn't laughed so hard in weeks, and she was aware that Lex, next to her, was laughing too. It was a shock to realise that she had never yet seen or heard him laugh out loud. While they were here, for this short time, he seemed to have forgotten everything.

He was still smiling as they emerged from the cinema. 'I don't feel like going home just yet,' he said. 'Would you like to go for a walk and have a drink some place?'

They had a leisurely stroll around town, not talking very much, but it was an easy silence. Coloured
lights were strung along bridges and buildings in
celebration of the tourist season, and it looked
cheerful and inviting. Tourists were everywhere
and Andrea heard snatches of conversations in a
variety of languages. Yesterday's rain had given way
to lovely weather and the evening was pleasantly
warm. They found a table at a sidewalk café that
was just being vacated by a German-speaking
couple.

There was a candle on the table throwing strange
shadows on Lex's face, making him look dark and
very mysterious. She'd wondered before if he had
gypsy blood, and now more than ever he looked as if
he did.

'Is there a gypsy somewhere in your family?' she
asked on impulse, and he gave a hearty laugh.

'Yes, I believe there was, way back. There are
rumours that one of my great-grandfathers was the
illegitimate son of one of a roving band of gypsies.'

'Sounds very romantic.'

'It probably wasn't for his mother.'

'No, I suppose not.'

A waiter appeared at their table. 'What would
you like to drink?' asked Lex.

'A glass of port would be nice. Sweet.'

Their talk was light and easy and she liked it that
way. She felt happy—a kind of happiness she hadn't
felt for a long time. She didn't want to go home. All
she wanted right now was to sit here and drink another glass of wine and watch the tourists passing
by, watch Lex and listen to him talk.

Only he didn't talk very much. She watched him,

not seeing the people around them any more, not
hearing the conversations at the other tables. She
was only aware of him now and a strange emotion
filled her.

She wanted to touch him. She looked at his hands,
large and brown, and she wanted very much for him
to take her hand in his. But he had not touched her
all that evening, and she knew he wasn't going to
touch her now.

Later that evening she lay in bed, wondering
about him, seeing again his laughing face, wondering
again what it would be like to have him make love
to her.

But after she fell asleep she dreamed about him
holding her hand as they walked along the canals,
just holding her hand and nothing else. She thought
about the dream when she woke up. It seemed a
very juvenile dream, like the kind she'd had when
she was fourteen or fifteen. All that day she thought
about the dream, until finally it occurred to her that
the holding of hands had nothing to do with sexual
desire, but symbolised a trust between them.

Trust. Why would Lex trust her? Why would he
open up and take her into his confidence? Why
would she want him to?

For the rest of the week she saw little of him, and
on Friday she came home from the office to find
him gone again for the weekend. She felt restless all
that evening. It bothered her to admit that she was
often thinking about Lex. She wondered vaguely if
she were falling in love with him. Of all the men she
had encountered in the last few years he was the
most unlikely prospect for an emotional attachment.
She was angry and irritated with herself for even
allowing herself to think along these lines.

Saturday morning she woke to a glorious day. She opened the window to let in fresh air (if there was such a thing, she thought wryly) and leaned on the windowsill to look down into the street. It was alive with traffic—cars, buses, bicycles. She could see the intersection, heard the warning clang of an approaching tram. Two dogs were fighting on the pavement. A flash of light hit her eye from across the street—the sun's reflection caught by an opening window. Someone had draped sheets and blankets over the windowsill to air them out.

After breakfast she went out to stock up on groceries for the next week, Lex's last weekend with her.

She could not bear the thought of having to spend the entire weekend alone in an empty apartment. There was nothing special to do; she had made no plans. So she got on a train to Tilburg and spent the weekend with her parents.

Monday was a hectic day at the office, with an unusual number of phone calls and a sick secretary. Andrea came home tired, wearily climbed the four flights of stairs, smelling the old lady's cooking—she couldn't identify what, and hearing Ria's baby crying again.

But it felt good to be home. Her apartment was like an oasis, clean and green and welcoming. And Lex was there in his room—as always, she could sense his presence.

She knocked on his door, wanting to say hello, but no answer came. Apprehension flooded her, a strange, frightening premonition. Quietly she opened the door and peeped in.

He sat slumped at the desk, his head on his arms. There was a bottle of *jenever* and a shot glass on the desk. Without thinking Andrea advanced into the room and touched his shoulder.

'Lex! Are you all right?'

He lifted his head and looked at her glassy-eyed, then recognition dawned.

'Leave me alone,' he said huskily. 'Just leave me alone!'

CHAPTER THREE

FOR a moment she stared at him, not moving. Then slowly she turned and left the room, closing the door quietly behind her. In the kitchen she sat down and tried to collect her thoughts.

It looked as though he'd spent the day drinking himself into a stupor. It made her furious and sad at the same time. The idea of a drunk in her attic did not appeal to her in the least, but the distress behind it all overrode her anger.

It was almost six and time to start dinner, but all hunger had vanished and she couldn't bring herself to even think about what to eat. What she wanted was a cup of coffee, hot and strong. Wouldn't do Lex any harm either if he ever surfaced from his room, which she doubted very much. Well, she would leave him alone. She knew better than to aggravate an intoxicated male.

The phone rang as she reached for the coffee. She put the canister down and lifted the receiver. It was Annette.

'My brother was here when I came home. Pieter, the one you met a couple of months ago, remember?'

Andrea remembered. A comedian, that one. One evening in his company was enough to remember him for a lifetime. The teasing never stopped, the jokes never ended. She smiled at the memory.

'I remember him, yes.'

'He's brought some take-out Chinese food—

enough for an army, and I thought maybe you'd like to come and join us. Afterwards we can go into town and have a drink somewhere.'

Why was she hesitating? She could do with a laugh, that was for sure, and Pieter would be supplying them all night. There was no reason whatever why she should stay home. With Lex drunk in his room she'd be better gone. His face floated in her mind's eye. He'd be sleeping for the rest of the night. He wanted to be left alone; he'd practically yelled at her to leave him alone. She closed her eyes briefly.

'I'd love to come, but I can't,' she said.

There was a short pause. 'What do you mean you can't? Just this afternoon you were telling me you weren't doing anything.'

'My room-mate is sick. I think I'd better stick around.'

Another silence. 'The guy who barged in on you a couple of weeks ago?'

'Right. He's feeling really lousy.' Andrea had made that up, but it was probably true, one way or another. 'I'd have loved to come, really.' Which was true. She hung up the phone, instantly angry at herself. Why did she have to do such a stupid thing? Why didn't she just go out and have a good time?

Coffee spilled as she spooned it into the coffee-maker, the grounds scattering all over the counter top. Sighing, she wiped them into the sink and rinsed them away. Something intangible, some instinct or premonition was telling her to stay home. She did not understand it. Feminine intuition? She shrugged as she plugged in the coffeemaker. She wasn't altogether sure there was such a thing.

I'm sorry for him, she thought, that's why I'm staying here. I'm sorry because I know he's miserable and alone and lonely and I know how it feels.

There's nothing you can do, another part of her said. He's a stranger. He hasn't confided in you. You know nothing about this man. You're not responsible for him. What are you thinking about?

I'm not thinking about anything. I'm staying home. There are lots of things to do. I can wash my hair, do my yoga, finish my book, clean the bathroom, write Sylvia a letter she won't easily forget.

Ten minutes later as she sat drinking her coffee, Lex emerged from his room. To her surprise he sat down in the chair facing her.

'The coffee smells good,' he said in perfectly enunciated tones.

'I'll pour you some.' She got up to do so.

He looked washed-out, the way he had looked last Monday week. His face was pale under his tan, with deep lines of fatigue around his mouth and eyes. It made Andrea wonder, once again, what he did and where he went on those weekends when he wasn't in Amsterdam. She wished she had the courage to ask.

She handed him his cup and he took an eager swallow, then he looked at her with an unreadable expression in his eyes.

'I'm not drunk,' he said. 'I imagine that's what you thought. I haven't been drunk since I was twenty or so. Maybe it would do me good to get good and sloshed some time.' His voice was dry.

Andrea said nothing. Yes, maybe it would do him good to get drunk, maybe it would do him good to let go and talk, maybe it would do him good to cry.

He looked as if he'd locked himself up in an emotional tomb. But it would never work. It hadn't worked for her. For months after Bart's death she had lived in numb, dull apathy, an emotional void, refusing to accept the truth, afraid that if she would let go of her control and give in to her locked-up emotions, they would be more than she could handle. But it had been impossible. A day had come when she no longer could bear the emotional emptiness she had created inside herself, and she had broken down, utterly and completely. It had struck her then, the final truth. *This is forever. Bart is dead.*

She had survived. But now, looking back, it was still very clear in her memory—all the despair and anguish and loneliness, and she could see them all reflected in Lex, in his eyes, his face, and in the things he left unsaid.

She wanted to reach out to him, to this man, this stranger. In a way the thought alone seemed preposterous. Who did she think she was? Why did she care?

'I fell asleep at the desk,' said Lex. 'All I had was one drink, but I was exhausted. I lay awake all last night.' He stared at some point beyond her shoulder, lost in thought.

Was he saying these things to put her at ease? Andrea wasn't sure. Her cup was empty and she replaced it on the table in front of her. What was he expecting from her? Did he want her to ask questions?

She looked at him and swallowed. 'I know you're going back to Bolivia next week. I hope there aren't any . . . any problems.' So, she had done it. She'd asked, or at least come as close as she dared to asking.

The silence seemed eternal and she became aware of an increasing feeling of apprehension. Lex's hands, resting on the armrests of the chair, were clenched into fists. Slowly, nervously, her eyes moved up to his face, seeing with painful shock the tormented look in his eyes.

'Lex. . . .' she whispered. 'Lex. . . .'

'I have a daughter,' he said then. His voice was strained, as if it took an effort to say the words.

For a moment she was stunned. It wasn't at all what she had expected him to say. A daughter . . . he had a daughter! She stared at him, amazed by this bit of information, amazed that he had actually told her something about his personal life.

'I didn't know.'

'No.' He was not looking at her. 'She had a birthday yesterday. Her sixth.'

'Where is she?'

'In Apeldoorn with my sister and her family. She started school this week, first grade. I'm going to have to leave her here.'

'Surely there are schools in Bolivia?'

'Not in that godforsaken place where I live.'

His cup rattled in its saucer and he deposited it on the table and stood up. He turned away from her, shoulders hunched, hands in his pockets.

'She's so damned happy! Living in one of those sterile row houses in one of those neat little streets. All the houses the same—blue doors, big glass windows with lacy curtains and a jungle of plants on the windowsills. And all those pathetic little squares of grass in front and back, and a trillion small kids on tricycles and bicycles and God knows what kind of plastic contraptions they have these days, and she *loves* it.'

Andrea stared at his back, the hunched shoulders, listened to the outpouring of his angry words, knowing it was only pain in disguise.

'Everything is perfect,' he said after a pause. There was bitterness in his voice and Andrea's heart contracted.

'Everything is perfect,' he repeated. 'My sister has a daughter the same age, two months apart they are, and they're like goddamn twins. They love each other. You should see that little room they share—bunk beds, and she loves it.'

'It sounds ideal to me,' Andrea said quietly. 'A good place for her to be if she can't be with you. You won't have to worry.'

He swung around, his dark eyes a painful blaze. 'Yes! Perfect! I'll go back to that damn hole and forget about her! She doesn't need me. She has all she needs right there in Apeldoorn—a family life, a makebelieve sister, love and care. What does she need me for? I'm no use to her!'

He moved away from the window and sank back down on the couch, lowering his head into his hands. Without thought Andrea got up from her chair and sat down next to him.

'It's only for the one school year. You told me you'd be finished with your work in Bolivia next summer. You'll be together again after that.'

He lifted his head and what she saw wrenched at her heart. His eyes were filled with a helpless misery, a silent despair.

'A year is too long,' he said thickly. 'I'll lose her too.'

I'll lose her too. He'd lost his wife through death.

Now he was afraid he'd lose his daughter's love through distance and circumstances. Maybe he was justified in his fear, she had no way of judging that.

There was nothing she could do, nothing she could say, and never before had she felt so helpless, so utterly helpless. She looked into his eyes, seeing nothing but a blind despair, and instinctively and without thought she reached out to him and put her arms around him. She had no words of comfort, only this primitive, silent gesture.

He sat still in her embrace, totally still. Her face touched his and for a long time they just sat there, silently, not moving.

He stirred at last, taking her face into his hands, looking into her eyes.

'Oh, Andrea,' he said softly, 'why do you bother with me?'

'I've done nothing.'

'But you have. You're always here, looking at me with those gentle eyes, asking no questions, but wondering all the time. Ready to come to my rescue with your quiet words and strong cups of coffee and your massage, and now . . . here you are, listening to me.'

'It's all right.' Her heart was thudding and a nervous shiver thrilled through her. She was suddenly aware of how close together they were. She could feel the warmth of his body against her own, and the feeling that stirred in her she didn't want to feel. It was too dangerous, much too dangerous at a time like this.

But his eyes held hers and she couldn't look away. The atmosphere changed, very subtly, and something surrounded them, enclosed them, blocked out the world. Her heart was racing, racing. . . .

Lex's face came closer, closer, and then he kissed her, as she had known he would. It was gentle and careful, but only for a moment, and then it changed until there was more than just a kiss. It was a searching and a hungry wandering of his hands, sliding over her, seeking, touching. . . . A desperate yearning overwhelmed her, a deep longing that had lain dormant for a very long time. Oh, God, she thought, oh, God . . . but it was too late now for coherent thought. She was trembling in his arms, responding, kissing him, touching him with a need of her own. There was nothing now but the two of them, the warmth of their bodies clinging together.

And then it was over, suddenly, disastrously, and she stared at his face that was ashen and the eyes filled with horror.

He was up and out the door before she could utter a sound. Her heart was beating so fast, she thought it might stop. Her legs were shaking as she rushed to the window. She looked down into the street and saw him cross over to the other side, head bent. He disappeared around the corner, and Andrea closed her eyes.

'Oh, God,' she moaned, 'how could I have let this happen?' There was an ache in her chest, a heavy, painful sadness. The knowledge was there inside her, undeniable.

He had been thinking about his wife when he had kissed her.

Half an hour passed. Andrea sat on the couch, not moving, staring blindly at the Monet reproduction on the wall—a wedding gift from friends. She thought of Lex wandering the streets somewhere. Maybe he was in a bar drinking himself into oblivion this time. She remembered his eyes when he looked up and saw her face and her heart shrank. And it was not because she did not understand, because she did. In the beginning it had happened to her, too. And she knew it was not anything personal to her; it had nothing to do with her, really. It had happened. He had kissed her, and she had wanted him to kiss her. Something was happening to her feelings for him, something potent and very confusing. Dear God, she thought, don't let me fall in love with him. He's not himself, and I don't know him at all. He's leaving next week, and it's all so hopelessly impossible.

I'm sorry for him, she thought for the second time that night. I'm sorry because I know what he's going through. But was that all?

No, that was not all. Restless, she stood up and walked back to the window. She pulled off a yellow leaf from the philodendron that climbed along the window frame. Her feelings confused her, amazed her. How could she not know? How could she be so unsure?

She did not understand. Her love for Bart she had never questioned. She had always been sure—always. She'd known him ever since she was a child. She'd known everything about him, including most of his girl-friends.

But this was different, so very different. On the surface they were nothing more than friendly strangers. Lex was a man with a whole life behind him, a wealth of experiences she knew nothing about—except the one he was struggling with now. And for reasons she didn't quite understand it seemed to create an invisible, intangible connection.

The doorbell rang, shattering her thoughts, and with a sigh she hurried out on to the landing and pulled the cord to open the front door. Voices drifted up from the entrance hall, and bending over the railing, Andrea peered down below.

'Andrea?'

It was Annette, and with her was Pieter. Inwardly Andrea groaned. She didn't want visitors now. She was in no mood to dispense the proper civilities, be polite, invite them in, offer them coffee. She wanted to be alone.

'Come on up!' she called down. What else could she do?

They were coming up the stairs, Pieter whistling. He was grinning as they reached her door.

He looked ludicrous with his striped jeans, the wide exotic orange shirt with purple embroidery, the black silk top hat and sunglasses. He clutched a bottle of wine against his chest and with his free hand he took off his hat and bowed deeply and pompously.

'We bring you instant joy and cheer, oh Majesty,' he said, handing her the bottle of wine.

Behind him, Annette sighed deeply. She gave him a little push. 'Oh, shut up, Pieter. Just go in.'

They did. Andrea went into the kitchen for glasses and a corkscrew, which she handed to Pieter.

Annette gave Andrea a quizzical look. 'Where's your friend? Is he in bed?'

'No. He's out.' She sounded short, but she couldn't help it.

'I see.' Annette looked at Pieter. 'What's the matter, can't you open a wine bottle?'

At last they were drinking the wine. Andrea wished they weren't going to stay all night. She hoped they'd leave soon. She felt ungrateful and ungracious, and guilty.

'Thank you for coming,' she said, forcing a smile. 'Thanks for the wine.'

'We're not staying,' Annette said decisively. 'Pieter just wanted to say hello, and since you couldn't join us for a drink in town, we thought we'd bring it to you.'

'And I wanted to tell you my newest Belgian joke,' he added with mock seriousness.

Annette groaned. 'Forget it, Pieter. It's as old as the road to Rome.'

'It is not! I just made it up this very afternoon!'

Annette shrugged and gave him an exasperated glare, then looked at Andrea. 'What he did was re-cycle a Polish joke from the States.'

'Okay, okay, forget it.' Pieter picked up the bottle and refilled the glasses. 'I know, dear sister, that you don't think I'm so funny, but at least I know there are *some* people who appreciate my talents.'

Annette grinned. 'You're right. Why don't you tell Andrea about it?'

'You do it. I don't want to brag.' He looked modest.

'He gave his first one-man show last week, at an old people's home in Groningen. It was a great success, and he's going to do more.'

'Hey, that's fantastic!' Andrea smiled with genuine appreciation. 'Congratulations!'

'Thank you.' He inclined his head graciously.

'He's not getting paid for it, though,' Annette commented dryly.

'Who needs money? Laughter is all the reward I want,' he said piously.

'Until they offer you money.'

'Right. Then I'll take it.'

His dream was to become a comedian, he had told Andrea. He was a student at the University of Groningen and had been for many years. 'The eternal student,' Annette had called him. 'If ever he gets out of there with a degree, it'll be a miracle!'

He worked on a student cabaret group with several of his friends, performing for his fellow students, but what he really wanted was his own show—theatre performances, TV.

An hour passed and finally they left. Andrea took her glass to the kitchen and dumped the wine. She was in no mood to drink. Two more hours went by and still Lex was not back. Where was he? Maybe he'd gone for a walk in Vondelpark. Maybe he'd got mugged. She laughed at the thought. People like Lex didn't get attacked; too tall, too big, too dangerous.

Dangerous? What made her think that? Powerful, yes. Strong, muscular, masculine, all that. But he was hardly dangerous. He was a man with problems and worries, a man fighting a crippling loneliness, a man in pain.

Back at the window she looked down into the street once more. So, she said to herself, what are you going to do about it? Are you his social worker? You're lonely too.

At this hour there wasn't much traffic any more. Some cars, a couple of bicycles, a few people walking their dogs. No Lex. She sighed and leaned her forehead against the cool glass and closed her eyes. Yes, she was lonely too. She had family and friends, but the closeness she had once shared with Bart was not replaced by anything else. There was still the void his death had left. She thought of Lex alone in the dark, of the wife he had lost, of the little girl he had to leave behind.

Drawing a deep, steadying breath, she turned away from the window. Taking the watering can to the kitchen, she filled it and began to water the plants. They didn't really need it, but it gave her something to do while she was waiting.

Waiting, she thought, and it was like a revelation. I'm always waiting. Waiting for him to come out of his room. Waiting for him to come back on Monday. Waiting for him to talk to me, to trust me.

Why did it matter so much? Why did she want him to trust her, to confide in her? She thought again of the dream—the dream that she was walking hand in hand with him.

And then she heard the steps outside the door and the key turning in the lock. The door opened and he was back. He looked dishevelled, his black hair falling untidily across his forehead, his face showing the dark growth of beard.

'I thought you'd be in bed by now.' His voice was level.

'I was waiting for you.' It was true and she wasn't going to pretend otherwise.

'You shouldn't have. I'm quite sober.'

Andrea gave no reply.

'I'm sorry about what happened. I lost my head.'

'It doesn't matter.'

'Yes, it does! I . . . Oh, what's the use?' He turned his back in a helpless gesture of defeat. She stood behind him, not touching.

'Don't you think I know? Don't you think I understand?'

He swung around. 'Understand what?'

'That it wasn't *me* you were holding in your arms. That it wasn't *me* you were kissing.' She held his gaze locked, refusing to turn away her eyes.

'Why didn't you stop me?'

'I . . . I didn't realise it until afterwards, when I saw the way you looked at me.'

'Oh, God,' he groaned. 'You don't deserve that, Andrea.'

'You talk as if you did it on purpose,' she said, trying to keep her voice steady.

He raked both hands through his hair. 'I haven't been within ten feet of a female in the last year, and now this.'

'It was bound to happen some time.' She took a deep breath. 'You can't play dead for ever, Lex.'

He gave a short, bitter laugh. 'I wasn't playing at it, believe me.'

'You can't suppress your emotions indefinitely. You'll have to own up to them sooner or later. You'll have to learn all over again how to live and laugh and . . . love.'

He closed his eyes. 'Spare me the platitudes,' he said wearily.

Anger flared through her, but only briefly. 'Words are all there is right now.'

He looked at her for a long moment, face expressionless. 'I'm sorry, I didn't mean to snap at you.'

'It doesn't matter.' She hesitated. 'I know how it feels, Lex. I know how it hurts. And what happened to you earlier this evening isn't so strange. It's happened to me, too—more than once.'

For a long time he looked at her silently, as if he searched for something in her face, as if he really saw her and wanted to know more.

'Did you love your husband?'

'Yes.' She met his eyes. 'Did you love your wife?'

'Yes.' He turned abruptly, as if he couldn't bear to discuss it. He was silent for a moment, then she heard him sigh heavily.

'Why do you bother with me, Andrea?' He had asked the same question earlier this evening, and now he was asking it again. There had to be an answer, for herself, for him.

She stared hard at his back, swallowing nervously. 'Maybe because . . . because you need me.' It took an effort to say the words and she couldn't have said them had she looked at his face instead of his back. He stood very still and fear swamped her. Of all the pretentious, preposterous things she'd ever said in her life. . . .

He turned slowly and looked at her with some unfathomable expression in his eyes.

'*Need you?*' he asked softly.

CHAPTER FOUR

TREMBLING all over, she looked straight into his eyes. She didn't care any more. 'Yes,' she said shakily, 'even big, tough, brilliant men like you sometimes need someone else, someone to help put things in perspective, someone to talk to. I may be young in your eyes, but . . . but I've done a little living and a lot of loving, and . . . and I lost my husband.' She paused, drawing a deep breath. 'I wanted to die too,' she added softly. 'Don't you think I understand?'

He stared at her silently, his expression shuttered.

Andrea took another deep breath and gathered her courage. She wasn't going to stop now, no matter what the consequences.

'You don't have to be so damned brave all the time, Lex. You have the right to your hurt and your pain. You're human like everyone else. It's not a crime to hurt. It's not a crime to cry. Maybe,' she said softly, 'maybe your problem is that you haven't cried enough. Big tough men don't cry, do they?'

'Shut up!' he said hoarsely, then turning on his heel, he strode into his room, slamming the door.

Her eyes fixed on the closed door, Andrea wondered from where she had got the nerve to say the things she had. But she wasn't sorry. And she wasn't finished, either. She opened the door and walked in.

He was lying on the bed, face down into the

pillow, his hands next to his head, clenching the pillow between his fingers. His body looked tense and rigid. Andrea walked up to the bed and put her hand on his back, but he gave no reaction. She had half expected him to lift his face and shout at her, to tell her to leave him alone.

Kneeling by the side of his bed, she moved her hand to his head, feeling the thick hair curling around her fingers. And still Lex said nothing, didn't lift his face. There was something terrible about the rigid immobility of his body. Sheer force of will kept him from giving in to his emotions, kept them in an iron grip.

'It's all right,' she whispered. 'Oh, Lex, it's all right.'

It was as if her words released the last vestiges of his control and a violent shudder ran through his body. His shoulders heaved.

She put her face against his head and her arm around his back, feeling the convulsive movement of his body against her own, and then she was crying too, hot tears stinging her eyes. She was over-whelmed by a nameless grief, and she didn't know if it was for him or for herself.

She was not aware of time passing. At some point she was conscious of the fact that both of them were quiet and she was still holding him and he had not sent her away. *He had not sent her away!* The know-ledge filled her with happiness, a joy she couldn't explain.

Lex began to stir, turning on to his side and pull-ing her into his arms. His eyes were closed and his face seemed calm now. Andrea looked at him for a long time, then closed her own eyes. He was so close and she wanted so very much to kiss him . . . soothe his pain and loneliness, but the memory of what had happened earlier that evening kept her from doing so.

He lay very quiet, breathing regularly, and after a while she began to wonder if he had fallen asleep. She opened her eyes to look at him and although his eyes were still closed, she could tell he was awake. She released herself from his embrace and quietly left the room.

In the kitchen she began to make coffee. Everything seemed unreal—the kitchen, the green Laura Ashley print tablecloth, the sugar bowl in her hand. She moved around as in a dream, not really knowing what she was doing. She heard Lex's door and he came into the kitchen. Taking a cup from her hand, he pulled her into his arms.

'I never met anyone like you,' he said softly. 'Never anyone like you.'

Then he kissed her, slowly, gently, then with less restraint. And this time there was no doubt that his kiss was meant for her, only her.

She kept her eyes down when he pulled away. Her heart was beating fast and she was afraid to look at him. Her reaction confused her. Not long ago she had stood in front of him, saying things she had no right to say, looking straight at him, nervous, but unafraid. She had boldly followed him into his room, put her arms around him, held him.

But this was different, so very different. It was part of something else and it frightened her.

He brushed her hair back over her shoulder and tilted her chin, then a faint smile turned the corner of his mouth. 'I'm hungry,' he said.

Relief flooded her. Hunger was something she

could cope with. She gave a shaky laugh.

'So am I.'

'I'll fix us an *uitsmijter*.' He turned and took ham and eggs from the refrigerator, found a frying pan and turned on the gas.

And so everything returned to normal. Andrea busied herself setting the table, finding bread and butter and pouring coffee.

'I have to go to Geneva for some meetings,' said Lex as he dished up the food. 'I'm leaving tomorrow morning and I'll be back on Wednesday.'

'Oh?' she said, surprised. 'I didn't know.'

'That's because I didn't tell you,' he countered dryly. He sat down, picked up knife and fork and began to eat.

Time was running out. He was leaving on Friday; that left only Wednesday and Thursday evening. Andrea sighed and began to eat.

'How about dinner on Thursday?' he asked moments later.

Dinner on Thursday. A farewell gesture?

She swallowed. 'I'd like that.'

Lex did not return on Wednesday as he had said. Coming home from work on Thursday, Andrea found the apartment still empty. Maybe he wasn't coming back at all. Maybe something had come up and time had run out.

Feeling dejected, she sat down at the small kitchen table. No last dinner together, not even a goodbye. He had left her life the way he had come into it: unexpectedly.

Almost seven. She might as well get herself something to eat, only she wasn't hungry. She got up and switched on the news on TV. Half way through, she heard the key in the lock and she jumped out of her chair, joy flooding her.

One glance at Lex's face and she knew he was in a mood that promised no good. He looked dangerously angry, his mouth a hard, straight line.

'What's happened?' she asked without thinking.

'Don't ask.' He marched into his room, kicking the door shut. A moment later it opened again and he stood in the doorway, tearing off his tie. 'We have a reservation for eight,' he threw out.

You can cancel it! Andrea swallowed the words just in time. She was suddenly furiously angry, but she restrained it with an effort. He had no right to speak to her in that tone of voice, and she had no intention at all of spending the evening with him while he was in a foul mood.

He was unbuttoning his shirt, still standing in the doorway, watching her. She saw his face and suddenly all anger melted away. There were deep lines of fatigue on his face and it looked as if he had had a gruelling day.

'We don't have to go,' she said, hearing her own voice, quiet, without a trace of anger. 'You look tired.'

He shook his head. 'I want to go. I'm sorry I was rude, Andrea. I don't usually take out my frustrations on innocent bystanders.'

'It doesn't matter. I can handle it.'

His lips quirked. 'So I noticed. Admirably so.'

'I'll go and change now. I'm sorry I'm not ready, but I wasn't expecting you any more.'

One black eyebrow rose in question. 'No? Do you think I would have left without saying goodbye?'

'I don't know.'

His anger seemed to have dissipated somewhat. She wondered what the reason had been, but she wasn't going to ask again. She went into her room, sat down on the bed, feeling sad and dispirited. She wanted to know what went on in his life, what made him angry, what made him happy. She wanted to know more about his wife and daughter, about his work among the Indians, but it was no use. Tomorrow he would leave, and most likely she would never see him again.

She rose to her feet and began to change.

Andrea had never been to Barbecue Castell before, and as they entered she looked around, seeing the large charcoal grill, the intimate bar, the fireplace with booths around it. Under any other circumstances, the warm, rustic atmosphere of the restaurant would have delighted her, but this evening she felt unaccountably sad. They sat down at their table, in leather chairs, and ordered drinks. The conversation was light. They talked about subjects and issues that didn't really matter, that didn't touch their lives in any significant way, and it was better so, because tomorrow Lex would be gone.

She glanced down at the menu. The words were dancing in front of her eyes and it had nothing to do with the drink. This would be their last evening together and it seemed to her an ordeal more than anything else. He had shared her attic for only a few weeks. A few weeks were nothing. *Nothing!*

She asked him to order for her and he gave her a searching look, then ordered grilled lobster for both of them, and a bottle of wine.

The food was probably the best she had ever eaten anywhere, but it gave her no joy. The wine failed to cheer her up. God, she thought, this is ridiculous. Eat, enjoy yourself. She took another bite of the lobster. It really was very good.

'Are you all right?'

Andrea looked up, to find Lex watching her. 'I'm fine.'

'Should I have ordered something else for you?'

'Oh, no! It's delicious. I'm sorry, I'm not being very stimulating company, am I?'

'You're usually quiet. I wonder sometimes what goes on in that head of yours.'

'Most of the time not very much.'

'And other times?'

'Profound thoughts,' she said, mocking herself.

'Of course.' He wiped his mouth on his napkin and finished his wine. 'Would you like dessert?'

Andrea looked at her plate. She had managed to finish her food, but no way could she eat anything else. 'No thanks, just coffee, please.'

The table was cleared and coffee was served.

He leaned forward, arms on the table. 'Andrea, has it been very difficult for you having me around these last few weeks? Talk about stimulating company—I certainly haven't been that!'

She looked at him for a long moment. How could she answer that? She couldn't think of anything very diplomatic.

'Well?'

She shook her head. 'It wasn't very easy,' she said truthfully. 'But I'm not sorry or angry or anything like that.'

'Sure?'

She nodded, and Lex took her hand and covered it with his own.

'It's been good for me being here with you. I wish I knew how to thank you.'

'It's all right, you don't need to.'

He squeezed her hand. 'Thank you just the same, Andrea. Thank you very much.'

She smiled at him uneasily, not knowing what to say. He released her hand and leaned back in his chair. He was watching her, contemplation in his eyes.

'Tell me about your husband,' he said after a pause.

His question surprised her. For some reason she was always surprised when Lex took an interest in her and her life. He seemed so consumed with his own, as if nothing else mattered in the whole world.

And now he wanted to know about Bart and she couldn't think of a thing to say. All that entered her mind was *I loved him*, as if that explained everything. Well, it did, didn't it? What did it matter that he'd been tall and blond and blue-eyed? That he'd been a soccer fan? It all seemed so insignificant.

'Don't you want to talk about him?' Lex asked gently.

She looked into his eyes. 'Oh, yes. It's just that . . . I'm not sure what it is you want to know.'

'Were you happy?'

'Oh, yes!'

'How long were you married?'

'Two years.'

'You must have been very young when you were married.'

'Nineteen. It didn't seem so young to me. I'd been

in love with him since I was fourteen, and it was awful.'

He laughed. 'Awful?'

'We were neighbours, and our parents were good friends. Bart was four years older and he just thought I was the nice kid next door. He was bringing girl-friends home all the time, and it made me miserable. They were all so pretty and sophisticated, at least I thought so.' She sighed, remembering. 'And I was nothing but a beanstalk. . . . Oh, I suffered!'

He gave a hearty laugh and shook his head with amusement. 'And then one day everything changed. . . .'

'Right.' Her cheeks grew warm, and it annoyed her.

He leaned forward, smiling into her eyes. 'And I don't want to hear a word about it.'

Some memories were special—too special to share with anyone, and he understood. Andrea was grate-ful for that.

'Would you like to get married again some day?'

She hesitated for a moment. 'What you don't have you can't lose.' She paused, meeting his eyes. 'I thought about it, these last years. About not loving again, not finding someone else and it would be easier in many ways, but it frightened me more.'

He did not respond.

'It's not easy, finding someone else.' She smiled. 'I'm very picky. I was spoiled.'

'What do you mean by that?'

She shrugged lightly. 'I had the very best, and that's what I want again. I don't want to settle for some mediocre relationship. Do I sound terribly greedy?'

'No, just sensible.'

'Sensible? Maybe romantic is a better word. I wonder sometimes if I'm realistic. If I want too much.'

He studied her for a moment. 'Do you think it's possible to love someone else again? To be happy with a different person?'

'I've got to believe it,' she said slowly. 'I don't know what I'd do if I couldn't believe that.'

He made no reply and for a while they were lost in their own thoughts. Then he straightened in his chair and looked at her.

'What kind of man was your husband? Did he put his feet up on the coffee table and drink beer?'

Andrea laughed. 'Oh, yes. While he watched soccer games on TV.'

'Nice and ordinary,' he commented.

'Of course, why not?'

'Because you're not ordinary.'

She was stunned for a moment. 'I'm as ordinary as they come,' she said then. 'In every possible way.'

His eyes held hers as he slowly shook his head. 'Oh, no,' he said softly. 'Not ordinary at all.'

Overwhelmed by a feeling she couldn't express, she couldn't think of a thing to say, not a single thing.

They walked back home, along the canals and across the bridges, lingering here and there. Andrea didn't want to go home; she didn't want him to leave. But there was nothing she could do, and she felt impatient with herself, because her feelings were irrational and she seemed unable to control them.

Back in the apartment, Lex wished her goodnight, giving her a brotherly kiss on her forehead. 'I'll see you in the morning.'

Andrea nodded. '*Ja. Welterusten.*' Her voice sounded odd. She turned and walked into her bedroom. It took a long time before she slept.

He had breakfast ready when she awoke next morning. He was dressed in his travel clothes and his suitcase stood near the door. He was going to spend the weekend with his daughter, he had told her, and on Monday he would leave for South America.

Andrea dreaded the thought of saying goodbye, and when the time came for her to leave to go to work, she was tense with nerves.

'I have to go now,' she said stiffly, 'or I'll be late.' Not that it mattered if she were late for once; she was always on time.

Lex stood up from his chair. 'Goodbye, Andrea. And thank you.' His voice was grave.

'Yes.' She swallowed. It was so awkward standing there, facing each other with all this space in between. She took a step forward and he reached out and she put her arms around him, holding him tightly, as if it were possible to restrain him, to keep him from leaving. But he *was* leaving, and. . . . She lifted her mouth to his and kissed him—fiercely, desperately, not knowing what made her do this, not caring.

'Andrea, please . . . don't. . . .'

She froze, feeling the blood draining from her face. 'I'm sorry,' she whispered, 'I'm sorry.'

'Don't apologise. There's nothing to apologise for.' Gently he took her arms from around his neck, held her hands in a warm grip and looked into her eyes.

'Andrea, you know what you were asking, don't you?' His voice was very gentle.

Her body tensed. 'I was asking nothing. *Nothing.*'

'No? Maybe not. You don't ask for much, do you? But you're ready to give it all—comfort, support . . . love.' His voice was very soft. 'But you need to receive it too, Andrea, even you with your calm eyes and gentle ways—so confident and secure and self-reliant. . . .' He searched her face and there was pain in his eyes. Slowly, very slowly he shook his head. 'Only I don't have it to give, Andrea—not now, not yet.'

'I know that . . . I know that. . . .' Her voice shook and she closed her eyes, pressing back tears. Lex put his hand on her head and gently pulled it on to his shoulder.

'You will find someone who can give you what you need, what you deserve. Just . . . don't ever settle for anyone mediocre. You are a very special person—loving, generous, and you deserve the best.'

He was saying goodbye, a real goodbye. His arms would never hold her again. Her throat ached, her eyes burned. He was going back to South America, far beyond her reach. He would be there with his pain and his loneliness. In time he would learn to live with his grief, and one day another woman would come into his life and he would be happy again.

Lifting her head from his shoulder, she searched for his face. 'Lex,' she said unsteadily, 'one day you'll be happy again.'

His smile was faint. 'I'll work on it.'

I wish I could make you happy. I wish I could be the one. But their lives were too different, too far apart.

He was so much older, and there was so much she didn't know about him.

She tried to smile, but it didn't work, didn't work at all. All she wanted now was to run away, but he was still holding her, not letting go. He drew her to him and kissed her, a brief gentle kiss that held no passion.

'Goodbye, Andrea.'

'*Dag . . . daag. . . .*' She turned and rushed out the door. Taking deep breaths, she ran down the stairs, fighting tears.

I'll survive, she told herself as she emerged into the sunfilled street. I've survived worse than this. I'll manage, I'll get over it.

But it was not easy living alone again, to come home knowing he was not there. Pieter came to Amsterdam again and asked her out. She accepted. An evening full of laughs—she needed it and she was grateful. There were other ways to kill the lonely hours; she had learned that once before, and she forced herself to stay active, not to sit around brooding, thinking.

A few weeks later Sylvia showed up again, with an enviable tan and blonde hair bleached almost white. For three days straight she talked of nothing else but her adventures in Vienna—the men she had met, the mishaps of her tourists, everything. Sylvia knew how to tell a story, although half of what she said was probably made up to make it more interesting. Andrea was glad to have her back. Life seemed more normal now.

'How did you get along with my cousin?' Sylvia asked one day while they were doing the dinner dishes.

'Fine.'

'Didn't you like him?'

'I liked him fine. He's a quiet person; I didn't see much of him.' Andrea dried a plate with great care.

Sylvia looked at her with speculation in her eyes. 'He's good-looking, isn't he?'

Andrea shrugged. 'I suppose so.'

'You weren't interested?'

Andrea sighed. 'It wouldn't have done me any good, Sylvia. From what I've heard and seen, he's in no condition to get himself involved with another woman.'

'You're right, I'm sorry.' Sylvia looked penitent. 'It was awful the way his wife died.'

He had not told her about that. The temptation was there, for a fleeting moment, to ask Sylvia about Lex, about his wife and what had happened. But another emotion was stronger and deeper.

She didn't want to talk about Lex. Not with anyone.

Autumn was miserable—rainy, windy and cold. Every night now Andrea would come home in the semi-dark and it was depressing. Life seemed a dreary routine. She longed for sunshine and warmth and laughter.

She began a new project, a patchwork bedspread in bright colours—oranges, yellows, some browns for contrast. It was something to do when she was home on the long winter evenings.

Sitting on the floor, she spread out the pieces and arranged them in colour patterns with a specific design. It would be easier that way.

'You'll never get it finished,' Sylvia predicted gloomily.

'You watch me!'

Sylvia sat curled up in the rattan chair with a book in her lap making a pretence of studying. She watched Andrea as she sorted through the pieces of material, searching for the right colour in the right place. 'I don't think you have enough fabric.'

'I know. I'll have to get some more.'

'You want to go to the Lapjesmarkt? I'll go with you!'

Sylvia was an open market enthusiast and Andrea too, enjoyed going once in a while. Going to the Textile Market was a good idea.

They had a hilarious time. The atmosphere at the market was one of boisterous good humour. Moving from stall to stall, they watched as old ladies searched through piles of pink lingerie for a slip or a night-gown that would fit, aided by enthusiastic vendors praising their wares. Expensively bejewelled matrons in fur coats dug their way through heaps of second-hand clothing. A young girl with long hair and a long skirt critically examined an old-fashioned tablecloth in gloomy colours.

'What do you think she's going to do with that?' Andrea asked.

'Make a long skirt out of it,' Sylvia said promptly. 'Or a coat.' She stopped in front of a stall where a secondhand fur coat on a hanger waited for a buyer. She took it off and tried it on. 'Wow, is this warm!'

Half a dozen onlookers shouted their comments in the earthy tones of the Amsterdam accent. Sylvia posed like a pro, swinging her long blonde hair and giving a toothpaste smile. The people loved it. So did the vendor, who promptly lowered the price to thirty guilders, saying the coat had been waiting just for her. 'You look like a film star, sweetheart,' he said, and the onlookers shouted their agreement.

They moved on without the coat. 'I almost bought it,' said Sylvia, laughing so hard she could barely get out the words.

Andrea grimaced. 'Yuk! Who knows what lives in that fur?'

Sylvia shrugged. 'You think everything is dirty. I could have it dry-cleaned, you know.' She stopped at a stall full of fabric remnants. 'Here, straight from the factory,' she said dryly, 'sterile.'

Andrea ended up with quite a selection of fabric, all in the right colours. The bedspread would be beautiful—in her mind she could see it finished on the bed.

'I'm hungry,' said Sylvia. 'Let's have something to eat.' They struggled their way out of the market and found a cosy little restaurant full of people, laughter and warmth.

Sylvia shook off her jacket and shivered. 'Boy, was it cold outside! I should have bought that fur coat.'

Andrea did not react. She studied the menu, which was short and basic.

'I'll have a couple of meat croquettes with bread and coffee. What do you want?'

Sylvia was rubbing her hands. 'Something hot and steamy. Do they have split pea soup?'

'Yes. "Homemade, thick and tasty," it says. Sounds good. I'll have that too.' She closed the menu.

The *snert* was very hot and very good, and it warmed them right up. It was with great reluctance that they finally got up and went back out into the cold.

Andrea spent the evening alone, piecing together

her quilt, thinking about Lex. Would she ever really forget him?

It was November and the city had come alive with colourful lights and brightly decorated store windows. All this in honour of Sinterklaas who arrived from Spain on a big white boat with bags and bags of presents for all the children who had been good throughout the year. There was a parade in the city, headed by the bearded old bishop in his long red robe and carrying a fancy mitre. Sitting majestically on his white horse, he waved and nodded benevolently to the crowds of children and adults.

December the fifth was the big day. Andrea could feel the anticipation in the air, but wasn't affected by it. It was a weekday, meaning she couldn't go home to her parents and celebrate. It would have to wait till the weekend, and it wouldn't be the same.

As a child she had been wild with anticipation, full of hopes for dolls, a bike, or other toys. She still remembered, the images of the past vivid in her mind. Her shoe was ready in front of the oil-burning stove, a saucer with sugar cubes for the horse next to it. Together with her sister she sat on her knees and sang all the Sinterklaas songs she knew, hoping he would hear. The ritual over, she crawled into bed, shivering with delicious excitement. If she could stay awake long enough maybe she could hear or see something. But she never did.

After Sinterklaas had departed for his native Spain, the weather turned colder and wetter. Andrea went home to her parents for Christmas and New Year's Eve, returning to a grey, foggy Amsterdam. The Christmas decorations were gone. Sylvia was

gone; she had a tour assignment for most of January
and had left for the sunny slopes of a ski resort in
Switzerland.

There was a lot of work to do that first day back
in the office. The applications were in and ready to
be read and evaluated, a job Andrea enjoyed doing.
Grateful for the load of work, she dived right in and
the day went by quickly.

The mood did not stay with her. Leaving the
office, she stepped out into a dark, wet night. Was it
never going to end? She walked along the canal, the
water glinting darkly, and across the bridge to the
tram stop. Several people were waiting, huddled in
their coats, hands deep in their pockets. The tram
was late. When finally it came it was so full they
could barely squeeze in. Hanging on to a strap,
Andrea thanked her lucky stars she didn't have far
to go.

An icy wind tugged at her as she stepped into the
street and within seconds she was chilled to the bone
once more. Despite her boots, her feet were wet and
cold and she shivered miserably as she quickly
crossed the street and turned the corner, hugging
her coat around her.

With stiff fingers she turned the key in the front
door and started up the first flight of stairs. It was
dark and gloomy and full of the smells of stale cooking. Cabbage. The old lady on the second floor
seemed to survive on cabbage alone—breakfast,
lunch and dinner. Passing Ria's apartment, she
heard the baby crying again. With legs that felt like
lead, she began the last flight of stairs. She was tired
and depressed. January and February were the worst
months of the year. They stretched ahead like a
never-ending sea of grey.

With the key ready in her hand, she stopped and stared. Her door was slightly ajar. Something stirred—a thought, a memory.

But oddly enough, no fear. No fear at all.

CHAPTER FIVE

HESITATING not a moment, she pushed open the door and went in. He was there, sitting on the couch, reading *Het Parool*. Slowly he lowered the newspaper and smiled.

'Hello, Andrea.' He spoke as if it were the most ordinary thing for him to sit there and greet her. She stared at him, speechless for a moment, seeing the face she remembered so well, the dark hair silvering at the sides.

'Lex!' Hastily she threw coat and gloves on a chair. 'Lex!' she repeated, aware she was grinning stupidly. Depression lifted like fog and joy rushed through her.

He came to his feet, as she moved forward, her hand extended. He took it in both of his, then drew her to him.

'I'm not going to stand here shaking hands with you,' he said in her ear. He kissed her very determinedly on the mouth, and it was as if a tidal wave struck her. Her arms came up around him and she responded to his kiss with reckless abandon, aware only of a potent sense of exhilaration, a joy that needed to be expressed.

He smiled into her eyes when finally he stepped back. 'Well, that was a nice welcome,' he said lightly, then laughed out loud when he saw the blood rising in her face. 'Suppose you can tolerate my company for a few days?'

He was staying!

'Oh, yes, of course!'

He grinned. 'I happen to know that my dear cousin Sylvia is away at the moment. A ski tour in Switzerland, I believe.'

'She gave you her key again, didn't she? She didn't tell me about it.'

'I told her not to. I wanted to surprise you. Mostly I wanted to see your reaction.'

'You got it.' Her cheeks grew warm again.

'So I did.' There was humour in his voice. He lowered his big frame into the creaky rattan chair and stretched out his legs. Andrea sat down too, her eyes not leaving his face. Was he really here? Or was this one of those deceptive dreams that seemed so very real and natural?

'I thought you wouldn't be back in Holland until summer. Did something happen? Is your daughter all right?'

His eyes were warm. 'She's fine. I just wanted to spend Christmas with her. I decided a year was too long to be separated from her.'

'*I'll lose her too.*' She remembered the anguish in his voice when he had spoken the words last summer. The loneliness must have been terrible for him these last few months—no wife, no daughter, only the memories, and the knowledge that his little girl was far out of reach.

'And it would give me the opportunity to follow up on some business here,' he continued. 'I have two meetings tomorrow, and this weekend I'd like to spend with you, if that's possible.'

'I'd like that,' she said, trying to sound calm. Oh, she liked it all right!

'You didn't have any plans for the weekend, then?'

She shook her head. 'Nothing special.' Nothing that mattered, nothing that couldn't be changed.

'Good. I was hoping for that.' He jumped to his feet with amazing agility. 'Now, how would you like it if I fixed dinner? I brought steaks, lettuce, French bread, and wine. Will that do?'

It was a wonderful dinner, better than anything in a restaurant, because Lex had prepared it, here in her green kitchen. Andrea let out a sigh of contentment. 'It is so nice, coming home to this, having you here to eat with.'

He was smiling, looking at her as if the sight of her pleased him. She felt so happy she wanted to hug him. The elation, the exuberance of her feelings made her restless. She wanted to jump up, put her arms around him, tell him she was so glad he'd come back. But the calmer side of her nature made her stay right where she was.

'I was so depressed when I came home,' she said. 'I hate winter, it's so damp and foggy and cold. I stood around forever waiting for a tram and my toes were frozen and when it finally came it was crammed full and I had to stand hanging on to a strap.'

'Then I've done my good deed for the day—cheered you up.'

To say the least, she thought.

'More wine?'

She watched as he filled her glass, seeing the strong brown hand holding the bottle. It was a good hand, big and well shaped, a hand to hold on to . . . if ever it were offered. She took the last bite of steak and chewed it slowly. Finished, she pushed aside the plate and straightened in her chair.

'How's your daughter?'

Martha was fine, he said—doing well in school,

overjoyed to see her father. He was glowing as he told her and she was warmed by the light in his eyes. He seemed so much happier than last summer.

He was going to resign when his contract was up this summer, he told her. He wanted to come back to Holland. 'I'll find a job, get a house and give Martha a little stability. These last few years have been hard on her, she needs some security.'

They had been hard on him too, no doubt, but he wasn't talking about that. Once more Andrea realised how little she knew about him, how little he had ever told her. She studied him in silence as he finished his wine, and he was watching her, too, smiling.

'What are you thinking?' he asked.

'That you've changed.'

'In what way?'

'You're not so morose and depressed any more. You seem more relaxed.'

He reached across the table and took her hand. 'Maybe because I'm not so unhappy any more,' he said slowly. 'Time has passed, and I've done a lot of thinking since last August.' His eyes held hers and something stretched between them—a feeling that knew no words, quivering in the silence.

At last he released her hand and pushed back his chair. 'Come on, we'll do the dishes. I'd considered going out to eat, but I'm glad we didn't.' He began to stack the plates.

'So am I. I like being home, especially with weather like this.' Andrea filled the dishpan with hot water and squeezed in some detergent.

'You're a homebody, aren't you?'

She lowered the wine glasses into the sudsy water and shrugged. 'I suppose I am.' Friends had warned her, saying it was no way to catch a man. But she wasn't going to hunt around at parties and in bars to find one, if that's what it took. She needed someone like Lex, who presented himself at her door.

He gave her a gentle push. 'Here, let me wash. You dry.' He handed her the towel.

The dishes finished, they made coffee and took their cups to the living room.

'How about some music?' He moved over to the stereo, and searched through her records, shaking his head. 'Such a romantic soul ... Sinatra, Aznavour, Nana Mouskouri. . . .'

'I have classical music as well,' she defended. 'Did you come here to analyse my personality? I'm not sure I want to listen to that.'

'No?' He put some records on the turntable and a moment later light piano music rippled around them. He sat down next to her, stretching out his legs. His eyes were laughing into hers. 'But I haven't finished yet. There's lots more I'd like to say about you.'

'You hardly know me.'

'That's what you think. I probably know you a whole lot better than you imagine.'

Andrea wondered what exactly he thought of her, how he saw her. A romantic homebody? It was hardly exciting. Well, she wasn't an exciting person, he should know that by now. The weeks he had spent with her last summer had taken on a strangeness in her memory, a kind of unreality, and now that he was here again it seemed stranger, because he had changed and didn't quite look like the man she remembered. The empty look had left his eyes and he was smiling, talking.

'More coffee?' He held out his hand for her cup.

'Please. You're quite domesticated, aren't you? Cooking dinner, helping with the dishes.'

He laughed. 'I grew up with three sisters, who insisted I do my fair share. I had less chance than a penny on a tram rail!' He strode around the divider to fill the cups.

'I used to do that,' said Andrea as he came back, 'put pennies on the tram rail, I mean. I was fascinated by the way they flattened out.' It seemed a long time since she'd been a child, a long time since she'd played hopscotch, hide and seek, marbles. A memory surfaced and she smiled. 'Do you remember those old-fashioned mail boxes we used to have? Those huge red ornamental monstrosities?'

He nodded. 'Yes.'

'One day, I was only six or so, I climbed on top of one. It was at the end of our street and I passed it every day when I went to school. I don't know how I managed, but I still remember sitting there, surveying the world. It was so strange. Everything looked different. And then this old lady with a raincoat on and a shopping bag stopped and started yelling at me to come down.'

'And you clambered down and ran home.'

'Absolutely not! I just sat there staring down at her thinking I was bigger than she was and there was nothing she could do to me. I felt inviolate, unconquerable, and it was the most wonderful feeling I'd ever had. I remember her face. I remember she had on a scarf, pink with red roses—gaudy.'

Lex laughed, amazement in his eyes. 'I have to admit I don't quite see you sitting on top of a mail box defying authority. So what happened?'

'She started yelling harder, telling me she was

going to call the police, and I still said nothing, just stared down at her. I wasn't scared at all. She was so mad, she would have dragged me down if she could have reached me. Finally she quit and walked off telling me she was going to call the police. When she was out of sight I climbed down and went home. But I'll never forget that feeling of total control. It was wonderful.'

'Mmm . . . power-hungry, huh?'

'No . . . it wasn't that.' Andrea frowned. His comment made her think for a moment. 'No, I just wanted to be independent, in charge of my own life. I never liked people pushing me around.'

He didn't comment on that, but there was a light in his eyes as he studied her face.

'Did you grow up here in Amsterdam?' he asked after a moment.

She nodded. 'Yes, but later my parents moved to Tilburg, that's where they're from originally.'

'You once told me you have a sister. Any more sisters? Brothers?'

She laughed. 'See? You don't know anything about me!'

'I know most of what counts,' he said slowly. 'But you're right, there are many things I don't know. Maybe this weekend I'll find out some more about you.'

The look in his eyes made her heart skip a beat. On the surface they were having a perfectly normal, quiet kind of conversation, but she was aware of an undercurrent that left her with a feverish sensation.

'Well,' she said lightly, 'I'll tell you one thing— my favourite colour is green.'

Lex groaned. 'That I knew even before I set eyes on you. And I just remembered, I have something for you.' He jumped to his feet, strode into his room—Sylvia's room—and came back a moment later with something small in his hand, wrapped in tissue paper.

He gave it to her. It was heavy and odd-shaped. Removing the tissue paper, Andrea laughed when she saw what she held in her hand.

A small green ceramic frog. It looked very real, its eyes made of some shiny stones that seemed to look right at her.

'I found it in an out-of-the-way little shop in La Paz. There was just one. It made me think of you.'

'Thanks a lot!'

He grinned. 'The *colour* made me think of you. The little monster himself reminded me of myself.'

Andrea frowned. 'Explain that.'

'Never mind.'

One glance at him and she knew he did not intend to elaborate.

He didn't want to talk about himself she realised after a while. He wanted to know about her. And she sat next to him on the couch, talking, holding the little frog in her hands, touching it, feeling it as she told him things about her life she didn't easily divulge to anyone. She found herself talking to him about Bart, about the love she had felt for him, and the memories of their two years together.

The thought crossed her mind that it was unusual for her to talk so much about herself, her life, her marriage. She was aware that his eyes never left her face as she talked. It seemed easy to open herself up to him. It felt right and good.

'You must have got married right after you came back from California,' he commented.

'Within a month.' She smiled. 'My poor parents!

They'd been so relieved when I got that scholarship, thinking it would be good for me to be away for a year, have some new experiences, get my emotions sorted out, get over this infatuation, etcetera, etcetera.' She laughed. 'It didn't work at all. I came back home, and there he was, waiting for me at the airport, and whammo!'

'You're good at knowing what you want, aren't you?'

She gave a light shrug. 'Sometimes.'

'Mmm, most of the time, I think.' Lex searched her face for a long moment. 'I haven't asked yet, but I need to know. Is there anyone who'd object to my being here with you this weekend?'

'Meaning, is there a man in my life?'

He gave a crooked smile. 'You like to have it straightforward and out in the open, don't you?'

'Right. And no, there isn't anyone special.'

There was a silence and she wondered why he had come to see her. Hope lay warm inside her. This wasn't just a courtesy call, that was obvious enough.

'I've been talking all evening,' she said then. 'Why are you asking me all these questions?'

He looked at her sideways. 'I've thought about you a lot these last few months. In a special sort of way it seemed I knew you very well, but in other ways I knew very little about you. You were a mystrery. You fascinated me.'

She was stunned by his reply. She *fascinated* him? Earlier this evening she had imagined he thought of her as a romantic homebody. Nice maybe, but boring.

She sighed. 'I'm not mysterious *or* fascinating, I thought you knew that.'

'That's not for you to decide, is it?' he asked, coming to his feet and pulling her with him. She was in his arms and his face was close, very close. He looked into her eyes and she grew still under his regard. Her heart began to beat wildly as sweet excitement flooded her. She closed her eyes and the next moment there was the feel of his lips brushing her mouth, warm, intoxicating. Her arms moved up around him and he pressed her closer against him in response. His mouth grew firmer and he was kissing her as he had never kissed her before, and her senses reeled. She responded instinctively, returning his kiss with a strange kind of desperation mingled with a fierce joy. It overwhelmed her, overpowered all restraint and gave free rein to her feelings.

She was dazed and breathless when finally he relaxed his hold on her. She held on to him, afraid he would let go of her entirely, but his arms stayed around her. For a long, vibrating moment he stared at her, then his mouth twitched into a smile.

'A warm-blooded woman under that soft, gentle exterior,' he said slowly, his dark eyes filled with an expression she couldn't read.

Warmth rushed into her cheeks. 'I'm sorry,' she said unsteadily. 'I got carried away.'

He laughed softly. 'It's dangerous, you realise that? Could get you into trouble.'

Yes, she knew. She knew very well. She took a deep breath. 'I can take care of myself,' she said with as much control as she could muster. But the words sounded hollow, even though they were true— most of the time. But now she was not so sure.

And he knew it too, she could tell by the expression on his face, and suddenly she was afraid. She didn't understand why, or maybe she did. He'd

brought her back to life by his touch, made her feel
again, made her want to be held and kissed and
made love to. All those emotions that she'd been
incapable of feeling for so long. It was wonderful
and frightening and she couldn't trust herself any
more. She didn't like to feel so vulnerable.

He said nothing, looking at her, knowing. She
freed herself from his embrace, feeling the weakness
of her legs as she stepped away from him. 'I'm going
to bed,' she said shakily. But before she could make
another move he had pulled her back into his arms
and was kissing her again, and she wanted him to
and yet she didn't. . . . It was going too fast, too fast
for her to grasp all at once.

'Don't,' she whispered against his mouth. 'Please,
Lex, don't. . . .'

He let her go, looked at her, eyes dark. 'I'm sorry,'
he said slowly. 'I'm not being fair. It's . . . been a
while.'

'I'm sorry . . . I. . . .'

He put his hand over her mouth. 'Don't,' he said
quietly, 'don't you dare apologise.'

She took a step backward. 'I'm going now.'

He nodded. 'Yes, and you'd better go quick.' His
voice was uneven and she saw what was in his eyes.
She fled.

A nightmare. Her whole body ached and she didn't
know where she was. As she looked around, everything swam around her and she could not bring
anything into focus. Trying to lift her head, she
moaned in pain and dropped back down on the
pillow. Her throat was dry and when she swallowed
it was agony. A convulsive shiver ran through her
and she was freezing cold. She pulled the covers up

to her chin and huddled under them.

A sudden hard ringing screamed through her brain. Automatically her hand moved and grabbed the little alarm clock and silenced it.

She was awake. She was in her own bed. There was no nightmare. The misery she was feeling was a painful reality.

I'm sick, she thought with shocked disbelief. I can't be sick! I'm never sick! Her hand touched her forehead. She was very hot and very woozy. A fever—the 'flu. It couldn't be! She never had 'flu! The worst thing she ever got was a head cold.

With sudden alarm she thought of the pile of applications on her desk, of all the interviews to be scheduled. She swallowed and winced.

Very carefully she sat up in bed. For a few minutes she sat very quietly, steadying herself, focussing her eyes. She was okay. Now, first her legs over the edge. Her feet touched the carpeting and slowly she stood up, holding on to a chair. A little dizzy, but otherwise she was fine. Her bones ached, but after she moved around a bit that should clear up. She could take aspirin.

Lex. He was here! She remembered he was here. He'd come last night. Or was it part of a dream? She couldn't think clearly and she wasn't sure. There was something about a little green frog. *A frog?* Her imagination, no doubt. Her brain was befuddled by the fever. Aspirin. There was a bottle in the bathroom.

Carefully she shuffled out the door and through the living room, holding on to various pieces of furniture. Suddenly Lex appeared in front of her, coming from the kitchen. Was he real?

'*Goeiemorgen*,' she whispered, leaning weakly

against the partition.

'Good God, what's wrong!' He reached out for her and just as his hands touched her shoulders blackness engulfed her.

When she came to she was lying on her bed and Lex was leaning over her. She stared at him for a full minute.

'Don't tell me,' she whispered. 'I fainted.'

'You fainted.'

'I've never fainted in my life! Never in my entire life!'

'Think of it as a new experience,' he said, lightly mocking her.

'You don't understand!' She was angry now, really angry. 'I'm not one of those females who go fainting all over the place!'

He laughed out loud. 'It's not a crime. It's simply the temporary loss of consciousness due to lack of oxygen to the brain. You. . . .'

'I don't want a medical lecture!' she whispered fiercely. Her throat was very painful and talking didn't help. 'All I want is some aspirin and then I'll be fine.'

'I want to have a look at you first,' he said calmly.

'Haven't you seen enough? I have a fever. I have a sore throat. I feel terrible. I fainted. I've got 'flu!'

'Or the onset of diphtheria or a streptococcus infection or. . . .'

She glared at him. 'You're not funny!'

'I'm not trying to be.'

Every bone in her body ached. She lay flat on her back, her pillow under her feet, and she was terribly uncomfortable.

'I want my pillow,' she demanded hoarsely, lifting

her head and reaching for it.

He pushed her back down as soon as she moved. 'No. You'll have to keep your feet up just a little while longer.'

Everything was swimming around again and she closed her eyes, but it only made it seem worse. 'I don't like this,' she whispered miserably. 'I don't like being sick. I'm never sick!'

'You're sick now,' he said calmly. 'And whether you like it or not you're going to stay in bed. The doctor says.'

'The doctor? Oh you. . . .'

'Me,' he acknowledged wryly. 'You could try to be more enthusiastic.'

'I feel awful. My throat hurts, everything hurts.'

'You have a flashlight somewhere? I'll have a look at your throat.'

'There's one in the kitchen drawer, the top one.'

'And a thermometer?'

'In the medicine cabinet in the bathroom.'

He looked into her throat for a long time, using a spoon as a tongue depresser. Andrea didn't like lying there with her mouth wide open. It was terribly inelegant. Not that she felt particularly elegant otherwise, wearing a cotton night shirt and with her hair all tangled from sleep.

He was feeling around her throat and ears with cool, firm fingers, asking her calm medical questions she didn't feel like answering. He was acting the perfectly calm, professional physician, and she resented it for reasons she didn't understand. All that was missing was the white coat and the stethoscope. Good thing he didn't have that, or she'd be lying there naked while he did his explorations of her chest.

His cool fingers felt good on her warm skin. Going

by the way she felt, her glands were probably swollen to the size of lemons. They were painful as he touched them.

He took her temperature and the thermometer registered forty degrees Celsius. From his expression it wasn't much to worry about.

'Looks like 'flu,' he said at last. 'You'll survive. Or in more medical terms: the prognosis is excellent.'

'I told you so,' she whispered. 'Besides, as a baby I was immunised against diphtheria. You should know that.'

He was looking down on her, smiling indulgently. 'A good doctor never takes anything for granted,' he countered smoothly. 'And now that we've established that you're not in mortal danger for the moment, we'll proceed with the treatment.'

'Which is what?'

'Bed rest, aspirin every four hours or as needed, lots of fluids, and me!'

'You?'

'I'm a very good nurse, believe it or not.'

'Maybe, if you give me some aspirin, I'll be all right. There's so much work and I really should get to the office and. . . .'

'You're rambling. You have a fever and you're not well at all. You're going to stay right here, and that's the last word I want to hear about it!'

He was right. She was sick, but she was never sick, all she ever had was a cold now and then, or a headache, and she didn't like this feeling of helpless misery.

'I don't like it,' she moaned. 'I don't like feeling like this.'

Lex laughed. 'Of course you don't. What you don't like is to be helpless and dependent, isn't it?'

'I fought too hard not to be.' There were tears in her eyes and her head was swimming.

'There are times in everyone's life,' he said, 'when he or she needs someone else. Nobody is totally in charge and independent all the time.'

There was something familiar about those words. They struck something somewhere in the far recesses of her mind, but she couldn't grasp the significance.

'I'm thirsty. Can I have the aspirin now? And some water?'

He moved to the door. 'Coming up!'

Andrea dozed for the next couple of hours, her mind a kaleidoscope of confusing images produced by the fever.

It was almost ten when she woke up. She felt better, but she was sticky and uncomfortable from her fevered sleep. More than anything else she wanted to shower, brush her teeth, comb her hair.

Carefully she sat up in bed. She was fine—mind over matter. The door opened and Lex came in.

'You look better,' he commented.

'The aspirin helped.' She swung her legs out of bed. 'I want to go to the bathroom. After a shower I'll be my old self again.'

'Absolutely not.'

Andrea stared at him. 'What do you mean, *absolutely not*? Since when are you telling me what to do and what not to do?'

'Since you passed out in my arms this morning. I don't want you in the shower. If you faint again you could crack your head and then we'd really have trouble.'

'I won't faint again!'

'Who says?'

'*I* say!'

He gave her a long, exasperated look. 'Andrea, I don't believe this is you I'm talking to. What's happened to this cool, calm, quiet woman I used to know? You're like some obstinate, recalcitrant child, for Pete's sake!'

'I'm sorry,' she whispered angrily. 'I'm sorry I'm such a nuisance! Why don't you leave me alone? I can take care of myself!'

'I'm beginning to understand why you're never sick. God has mercy on the poor souls who'd have to take care of you.'

'Well, I didn't ask you to take care of me. And if you'll move, please, I'll go to the bathroom.'

He stepped aside, taking her arm as she passed him. Irritably she tried to shake it off, but he was holding on tight.

'Don't be stupid,' he said curtly. 'I want you out of the bathroom in three minutes flat. And you leave the door unlocked. If I hear the shower, I'll come in and drag you out.'

She was defeated and she knew it, but her unhappy misery needed venting.

'I feel dirty. I'm sticky and sweaty and I want to wash!'

'You can do it in bed. I'll bring you a bowl of water, just like in the hospital.'

'I've never been in a hospital.'

'Take care you don't end up in one. Believe me, with someone like you the nurses show no mercy.'

'For a doctor you have a rotten bedside manner!'

He grinned. 'Depends on my patient.' He pushed the bathroom door open. 'Now, be careful. I'll be right out here, and I'll give you three minutes.'

Back in bed, Andrea had to admit to herself she was in no shape to stand on her feet for any length of time. How could she possibly get so weak in a matter of hours? She lay back, exhausted.

Lex came in with a bowl of water, soap and a towel.

'Can you manage? Or shall I give you a hand? I'm sure I can figure out how to give you a nice wash.' His voice was lightly mocking and she opened her eyes and glared at him.

'I'm sure you could, but no, thanks, I'll manage.'

He left the room, grinning, saying he'd make her some tea.

Nothing could beat a shower, she thought irritably as she wiped away with a wet flannel. She didn't like washing this way. She was sure she was not getting the soap off her skin. But it was better than nothing.

She found a clean nightshirt in her drawer, a green and white stripe, and she pulled it over her head, sitting on the bed. She ran a comb through her hair and tied it back into a ponytail. In the hand mirror from her bag she examined herself, and decided she looked even worse than she felt. There was nothing she could do; she certainly wasn't in the mood for an overhaul with make-up. She could barely focus her eyes. She was sick, so what the hell. She closed her eyes and lay back again, feeling weak, hating herself for it.

Not much later Lex came in with a tray—tea, a rusk with strawberry jam. She was thirsty and hungry, and her stomach apparently had not been affected.

'Thank you,' she said, looking up at him, smiling.

'You're welcome,' he said levelly. 'Feeling better after your wash?'

She nodded. 'I'm sorry I'm so unbearable, but I

just can't help myself.'

'Don't worry, I can handle you. And I will.' He grinned. 'I'm tough.' He sat down on the only chair in the room, a cup of coffee in his hand. He surveyed her as she sat up, drinking her tea, and she was very much aware of his eyes. As she met his gaze, she noticed the humour.

'What's so funny?'

'Those nightgowns—sleep shirts, whatever you call those things. First a blue one, now a green one. They weren't designed to give a man thrills, I can assure you.'

'They're comfortable,' she said. 'And don't talk to me about thrills. I'm ill, remember?'

'How can I forget?' He was laughing and she felt like throwing something at him.

'I'm glad you find me amusing,' she said sarcastically. 'Although I haven't a clue why.'

'No? Mmm . . . well, I suppose it's the surprise. I didn't know this side of you. In a way I'm glad to find you're not quite as perfect as I seemed to remember, in control of yourself and the situation. You never lost your temper. You were so patient and considerate, I wanted to scream.'

Over the rim of her cup Andrea met his eyes.

'Well,' she said lightly, 'it's a good thing you came back for another look. Now you know what a monster I really am when my true nature surfaces.'

Lex didn't reply to that, just looked at her, and she felt suddenly very warm, a warmth that had nothing to do with the fever. She lowered her eyes to her rusk, and finished eating.

She was tired again. How could she be so tired and weak? she kept asking herself. One thing was sure—from now on she would show a little more sympathy for other 'flu victims. This was the pits.

For the rest of the day she was in bed, sleeping most of the time and being looked after with great care by Lex. Her mood was terrible and she treated him like a slave. The fact that he seemed to find it all very amusing only made her behaviour worse, but she had no idea why. He certainly didn't deserve it. He allowed her to sit in the living room for a while that evening, just for a change. She sat huddled in the corner of the couch, feeling miserable. Her nose had begun to run like a tap and she'd worked her way through an entire box of tissues.

He had put a pillow behind her back and an Afghan over her legs and now he was in the kitchen fixing her a hot toddy. He had wasted his entire day on her and all she did was complain. And then she remembered his appointments and that he hadn't kept them and guilt surfaced full force.

'Oh, Lex,' she exclaimed, taking the hot toddy from him, 'you didn't go to your meetings! I would have survived, you know!'

He shrugged, unconcerned. 'I postponed them till next week. No harm done, as long as you'll let me stay on for another week.'

'Another week? What about your flight back to Bolivia?'

'I cancelled it and reserved one for a week later. Stop worrying about it, will you?'

'I'm sorry, it's all because of me.' Her voice wobbled precariously. 'I've spoiled everything— your plans, this weekend. I feel awful.'

'There's another weekend coming up,' he said patiently. 'I'm not walking out of here until I've spent some time doing the town with you. Come on, drink up now.' He lowered himself to the floor in

front of the couch, leaning back on his arms, and
watched her.

'I'm taking up the whole couch this way.' Her
voice was oddly distorted by the congestion in her
head. 'Why don't you sit in a chair?'

'Because I want to sit here.'

There was no arguing with that. She took a careful
sip of her drink. It was very good and very hot. She
lowered the glass in her lap.

'Lex,' she said, 'I want you to go back to
Apeldoorn. There's no sense in you staying here
while I'm ill. I'll manage on my own and by the
end of next week I'll be fine and we can go out.'

'I'm staying right here.'

'You don't have to.'

'I want to, my sweet Andrea.' He sounded very
patient.

She swallowed painfully. 'But why?'

He moved forward, leaning his arms on the edge
of the couch, his face close to hers.

'Because you need me,' he said softly.

CHAPTER SIX

She stared at him without speaking, then turned her face to the wall so he wouldn't see the tears in her eyes. It was true. She needed him, she needed him badly, and not only because she was ill. She felt his hand taking hers in a firm grip, felt hot tears sliding down her face.

'You need me.' The words were like an echo from the past. Once she had said those same words to him. With an effort she controlled herself, taking a shaky breath and wiping her eyes. She turned to face him.

'You remembered,' she whispered.

'Every word, every gesture, every touch.'

Andrea lowered her eyes, seeing his big hand clasping hers. Even now she didn't know from where she'd got the courage to say those words to him, to do what she had done last summer. He had been little more than a silent, unhappy stranger and her words had been presumptuous, to say the very least. He could have ridiculed her for her audacity, cut her down with contempt, but he had not. He had needed her then, as she needed him now. She was ill. She was lonely living all by herself in this small attic apartment, lonely for a man to care for her again, to share her life, to hold her hand as he was doing now.

Lex's hand tightened on hers. 'I kept thinking about you these last few months, wondering why you put up with me last summer. All that patience and tolerance—it seemed strange somehow. I must have been the most morose, miserable, unsociable individual you'd ever encountered.'

Andrea looked up. 'Try unhappy.'

'And you know about unhappy.'

'Some.'

'But you learned how to deal with it, didn't you? I realised you knew something I didn't. You're courageous and strong, and there doesn't seem to be much bitterness or rancour in that generous little heart of yours. . . .'

She shook her head. 'Please, don't make me sound like some . . . some. . . .'

'Paragon of perfection? You're not. I noticed that today.' His eyes were laughing into hers for only a moment, then he grew serious again. 'The more I thought about you, Andrea, the more I realised what a weakling I was, wallowing in my own misery, making no real effort to pull myself together and go on with my life and. . . .'

'Do you think I didn't go through that? You didn't know me then, but I was in terrible shape, full of anger and bitterness. It took me a long time to pull myself together.' A black space in her memory, those days. Painful to remember, impossible to erase.

He smiled ruefully. 'I might never have at all, but you helped me, Andrea. You helped me where no one else could. And that's why I'm here. I wanted to see you again.' His tone was soft now and she grew warm under his gaze. She lifted the glass and finished the hot toddy. He took the empty glass from her and put it down.

'It's time you got back to bed,' he said. 'You've been up long enough. How are you feeling?'

'Like a wet dishcloth.' She came to her feet, feeling

like a doddering old lady, her legs weak and shaky. Lex put an arm around her and led her into the bedroom. She turned towards him, putting her head against his chest, wanting him to hold her close, to feel the safety of his arms around her. He needed no asking. She closed her eyes, revelling in the feel of his strength and comfort and wishing futilely that she weren't ill.

'I'm sorry,' she murmured. 'I'm sorry I had to get the 'flu.'

'Think of it as divine intervention.' She recognised the humour in his voice, but it took her clouded brain a minute to catch the meaning.

'I'm sorry about that too, about last night. I acted like a silly teenager. I suppose you expected a little more sophistication from me.'

'I don't need sophistication,' he said quietly. 'All I want is to know how you really feel.'

'Did you know how I felt last night?' She was glad he couldn't see her face.

'Of course. You were very afraid of what you were feeling, and very confused. After all, you didn't even know I would be there when you came home.'

'I'm not very experienced in this sort of thing.'

He laughed. 'You were married for two years.'

'That's different. It's not what I mean.'

'No, you're right,' he said slowly. 'What you mean is that you haven't been sleeping around a lot.'

No, she thought, not a lot. Not *ever*. But she didn't say the words, instead she shook her head, her cheek rubbing against the roughness of his sweater.

Lex kissed the top of her head. 'Come on, I'll tuck you in and then I'll get you some more aspirin. I'll leave the door open tonight, just call if you want anything.'

Andrea lay in bed, thinking about the things he had said, thinking about how he had taken care of her all that day. It was wonderful to feel so cared for, not to have to worry about anything. She closed her eyes, snuggling deeper under the covers. He was here in her attic looking after her and she felt warm and safe. There was nothing to worry about, nothing at all.

He was there in her room when she awoke in the middle of the night feeling hot and very thirsty. He felt her head and gave her more aspirin and something to drink.

'I heard you toss around,' he said, 'so I thought I'd look in on you.'

She didn't want him to leave. She wanted him to stay with her and hold her hand. It was crazy, she was vaguely aware of that. I'm acting like a baby, she thought. I'm such a weakling. Is that what happens when your body collapses? But she wasn't like that. She was a strong person, she could take care of herself, she was in control of herself. But now she didn't feel like that at all.

Her dreams were strange and confused. It seemed that Lex was in her room again later, but she wasn't sure. She woke in the morning not feeling much better.

It took several days before the worst was over. He allowed her to take a shower and wash her hair. He had taken charge of her life completely and she had stopped fighting it after that first day. It was comfortable and safe to have him around, this big, dark mountain of a man.

As the days passed she became more aware of how much he had changed. She knew from the way he acted, from the things he said, that his deepest depression had lifted. There was laughter in his eyes now and his true nature, warm and loving, had taken over. Instinctively she had always known the kind of man he really was.

He opened up to her, seemed not nearly so uncommunicative as he had been, talking with ease now about his life, his daughter, his career. He explained in great detail the health and nutrition project he was working on in Bolivia—the successes, the setbacks, the seemingly insurmountable problems. Andrea listened with fascination, grateful to get to know him better. Her curiosity seemed insatiable.

They talked away many an hour. But never once did he mention his wife. And never once did she ask.

He often talked about his daughter and he seemed pleased with Andrea's interest. He produced a picture of her from his wallet and she took it from him to look at it closely. A mop of tangly auburn curls; big, bright eyes; a smiling mouth with two teeth missing in front. She looked as if she'd just come in from playing soccer. Andrea studied the picture for a long time. Except for the firm, proud chin, there wasn't much resemblance to Lex. Must look like her mother, she thought, and something contracted inside her. Was it pity for the child who'd lost her mother so early in life . . . or was it something else?

She handed the picture back. 'She's gorgeous,' she said truthfully. 'Looks very spontaneous.'

He laughed. 'Not a posed picture, you're right.'

'I'm glad you could spend Christmas with her. She hadn't forgotten you, had she?'

'No. My sister makes very sure of that.' He paused for a moment. 'I went to see her teacher to talk about her school work and she said she'd something special for me. It was a tape. She'd done an experiment in "public speaking" with her students. She'd told them to think about a subject they wanted to talk about—pets, vacations, hobbies, whatever, and then she recorded their presentations and made a big production out of it.'

'I bet half of them were too afraid to do it.'

'You're right.'

'But not Martha.'

He grinned. 'Not my girl!'

Andrea could see the love and the pride in his eyes. 'What did she talk about?'

The corner of his mouth lifted in a slight smile. 'Me.'

It made her happy to see him so pleased and proud. 'I hope it was the good stuff only,' she said lightly. She wished she could listen to the tape, hear what Martha had to say about her father, but she wouldn't ask. It was too personal, something between father and daughter. Envy surfaced unaccountably, and with it a sense of loneliness.

I want to be part of it, she thought. I want to belong and share what they have. But she was a bystander and there was no reason why she shouldn't be. Why then did she feel so shut out?

'Would you like to hear the tape?'

The question came unexpectedly. 'Oh, no! I mean, I don't think I should.' Had he read her thoughts?

'I have the tape with me. I'd like you to hear it.' His voice was perfectly sincere.

Andrea looked at him doubtfully. 'You mean it?'

'Yes, I do.' He went to his room to get the tape and Sylvia's little cassette recorder.

Martha's voice was clear and steady as she told

her audience that she wanted to talk about her father.

'My dad lives in Bolivia, and that's very far away. I lived there too, but now I can't because I have to go to school, so I live with my aunt and uncle and my cousin.'

Martha took a deep, audible breath, which made both of them smile.

'My dad is a doctor, but not the kind you go to here when you don't feel so good. He's a special kind of doctor. It's hard to explain. He . . . he . . . er . . . tries to make it so people don't get sick.'

Giggles from the classroom in the background.

'In this place where he works there are a lot of people who get sick a lot. There are a lot of Indians, but not the kind with feathers on their heads or anything. They're mostly just ordinary people. They wear long skirts and big hats and stuff. They're kind of poor, and they don't go to the doctor when they get sick because doctors are far away and most of 'em are scared of doctors, you know.' Another intake of breath followed by a momentary silence.

'The Indians don't have much food to eat, and some other people that work with my dad are helping 'em to grow more food so they can eat better. My dad says if you eat good food you won't get sick so much. Anyway, my Indian friend said that she didn't like that new stuff they were growing, so she won't eat it, and all she likes is potatoes.' Martha let out a deep sigh. 'I don't know what's going to happen. My dad is asking people to bring their babies and children so they can have injections so they won't get sick so much, but they don't like that either. My dad says they're afraid of injections because they think it's witchery or something. . . .'

Laughter from the classroom.

'It's not funny, you know!' Martha's voice was high with indignation and the laughter died down. 'Well,' she continued hesitantly, 'maybe it's *kind* of funny, except that my dad never laughed about that.'

Andrea stole a glance at Lex. Head bent, he was staring down at his folded hands, a smile creeping around his lips.

'So you see,' Martha concluded, 'my dad is really very special. My aunt talks about him a lot and she says I should be very proud of him. He's coming back this summer vacation and then we'll be together again.' A big sigh. 'I can't wait!'

Lex turned the tape recorder off and looked at Andrea with a faint smile. She wasn't sure if she could trust herself to speak. There had been no sentimentality in that little speech, but it had touched her deeply. As she had listened to Martha talk, she had almost seen her in her mind—the bright eyes, the vitality of her little face, the proud chin jutting out. A brave little girl, that Martha.

'She sounds very special herself,' she said at last.

His smile deepened. 'Of course. She's my daughter.'

She was up most of the day now, still sniffling and coughing a little, feeling hopelessly inelegant. This was not the way to lure a man. She saw her face in the mirror, pale, colourless, her eyes big. Her hair looked limp and lifeless, and she groaned in frustration. It wasn't fair. It wasn't fair! Why Lex hadn't fled days ago, she would never understand. But he didn't seem to mind, even seemed to get a certain kind of satisfaction out of caring for her.

'Aren't you bored?' she asked him. 'I'm not very inspiring company these days.'

He grinned. 'This wasn't exactly what I had in mind when I came here, but I have great hopes for improvement.'

Andrea sighed, and he laughed. 'Don't look so stricken! There'll come an end to this, believe it or not. You're looking a lot better already.'

'You mean to say I looked worse?'

'Much.'

How romantic could you get? She was angry, at herself and at him. 'I want to go out,' she said rebelliously. 'Go to a movie or something. I can't stand being locked up any longer. I'm getting claustrophobia!'

'Okay, tomorrow.'

'No. Tonight!'

'No, not tonight,' he answered calmly.

'But I'm bored! I've read a stack of books and magazines. I've been in bed enough to last me a lifetime. I want to do something!'

'All right, we'll do something.' He took her in his arms and kissed her forcefully. She pushed at him with all her might, out of sheer surprise. 'Don't! You'll get 'flu!'

'Not a chance. Doctors are immune, didn't you know? Besides, you're almost better, and I can't stand this any longer, either.' He continued where he left off, kissing her, touching her, until she thought her heart would stop. She was all aglow, feeling alive and full of love. She loved him. . . .

'Still bored?' he whispered in her ear.

'Don't tease me.' She had hardly enough breath to speak. His arms were around her, her head was on his shoulder and happiness suffused her. 'You're trying to take advantage of me because I'm weak and sick.'

'And you don't know how to handle men,' he added, silent laughter in his voice.

For a long moment she said nothing. 'Not someone like you,' she said then, her voice faint. She wasn't sure he had heard, because it was silent for what seemed like a long time.

'Andrea,' he said at last, 'I want you to understand that I didn't come here for a fast fling.'

'I know.'

'You'll believe me no matter what happens?'

Warmth flooded her. 'Yes.' How could she not believe him? How could he possibly think that she'd mistrust his motives after all he had said and done?

He lifted her chin to make her look at him. 'Thank you,' he said gravely. Then he smiled as his eyes moved over her face. 'Look what I did—brought colour back into your cheeks.'

'You're supposed to do that. You're my doctor.'

'Mmm, I don't think my methods are standard medical practice. But for you, of course, anything.' He nudged her gently. 'And now, to bed with you.'

The next day, Friday, she was as good as new, if still a little pale, but she could do something about that. After Lex had left for his meetings, she showered, washed her hair and blow-dried it. It looked nice—shiny again. Finding a pair of warm slacks and a wool sweater, she dressed. The blue matched her eyes and made them look bright. This weekend she was going to look good if it killed her. Lipstick, mascara, a touch of colour on her cheeks—it made a difference.

'Gorgeous,' she said to herself in the mirror, 'absolutely gorgeous. Or at least as close as I'll ever get,' she added with a sigh.

She felt wonderful, exhilarated and full of expectation, as if this were her first date ever. Nothing wrong in feeling that way, was there?

He's leaving on Sunday, a little inner voice warned. Don't get excited about nothing. There's no future in it—he'll be gone again for months. Forget it.

But she didn't want to. He was here now and she loved him, and that was all that mattered for the moment.

A knock on the door interrupted her thoughts. It was Ria, wearing shabby jeans and a sweater that had seen better days.

'Hello, Ria, come on in. Haven't seen you for a while.'

'Aren't you lucky?'

Andrea ignored the sarcasm. 'Sit down, I'll make some coffee.'

Ria did not sit down but followed her into the kitchenette. 'I saw him leave a while ago, so I thought I'd take my chance and come up and see you. He's been here all week, hasn't he?'

Andrea poured water in the coffee maker. 'Yes,' she said calmly, 'he has.'

'He's the same guy that was here last summer, isn't he? A gorgeous hunk of man for sure.' Envy coloured her voice.

Andrea's fingers clenched around the coffee canister. It irritated her beyond reason to hear Lex described that way. 'He's not a piece of meat, Ria, so for Pete's sake don't say idiotic things like that!'

Ria smiled, she actually smiled. 'In love, aren't you? Must have been a wonderful week.'

'Wonderful,' she returned dryly. 'Spent all week in bed.'

Ria stared at her wide-eyed. 'You're kidding me.'

'No, I'm not kidding you. I had a bad case of 'flu.' She took out cups and saucers, cream and sugar and put them on a tray. There were cookies somewhere, and she finally discovered them in the bread box where Lex must have put them.

'Come on,' she said, picking up the tray, 'let's go and sit in the living room. By the way, where's the baby?'

Ria sank into a chair with a sigh. 'My mother has him for the morning.'

'Nice. A little time to yourself will do you good.'

'I have a lot of time to myself, remember? I have a husband who's out with the boys every night, or that's what he says.' She took a sip from her cup. 'Your coffee is really good,' she said with feigned cheerfulness. 'So, tell me all about that Adonis of yours. I'm curious as hell.'

'I don't want to talk about him.'

Ria sighed. 'I was afraid not.'

She left an hour later with a cup of borrowed rice and some magazines Andrea had finished reading.

Lex returned late in the afternoon with a box containing two enormous pieces of *gebak*. Andrea groaned as she looked at the luscious fruit-and-cream-covered cakes.

'Don't you remember what your daughter said? This stuff is disastrous for your health. All that sugar . . .'

'If you don't want it, throw it out.'

'Never!'

'Good. No sense in being fanatics, now is there?

Besides, these are to celebrate your recovery. Come on, woman, make some tea, coffee, whatever.'

The restaurant he took her to later that evening was one of cosy comfort and the warm, intimate atmosphere enveloped her as soon as they stepped through the door. Soft piano music filled the air and she was delighted to see it was live—someone playing the piano. They were escorted to their table and ordered drinks. The beautifully set table was a joy to the eye—white tablecloth, silver cutlery, fresh flowers, soft lights shining on it all. Such luxury! She sighed involuntarily and Lex laughed.

'It's easy to make you happy,' he commented.

Easy? This meal was going to cost him a fortune.

His glance lingered on her face. 'You know what I like about you?'

'My nose?' Oh, that silly upturned nose!

'You have a cute little nose, nothing wrong with it.' A slight pause. 'What I like about you most is your eyes. They're really something, you know that?' He reached across the table and took her hand. 'They're clear and honest. That's what I like about you—you're straightforward with not a speck of deception in you. You don't pretend and you don't play games. You say exactly what you mean and I never have to second-guess you.'

Warmth spread all through her and she couldn't look away. 'Thank you.'

Lex smiled. 'Thank *you*.'

The food was delicious and they took their time over it, talking, watching the people who were dancing.

'Would you like to dance?' he asked when they had finished the main course. Her eager reply made him laugh and she felt silly and embarrassed.

They moved around as one. Closing her eyes, Andrea gave herself up to the feeling of utter happiness that flooded all through her—she belonged here, in his arms, safe and secure. She loved him so very much and she ached to tell him, but she knew she could not do that now.

Lex lowered his head to hers. 'I guess you like this kind of dancing,' he whispered in her ear.

She lifted her face to his. 'Actually,' she said lightly, 'I prefer disco.'

His mouth twitched in a smile. 'You're lying.'

'How would you know?'

'I just know.'

They had something light and luscious for dessert, something with a fancy French name Andrea forgot as soon as she'd ordered it. It was followed by strong coffee. She sat back and a sigh of contentment escaped her. Across the table was the man she loved. She looked at the familiar features, the dark hair beginning to grey on the sides, the eyes that had once been so bleak and now were looking at her with gentle laughter, and suddenly, from nowhere, depression swamped her. He was going to leave on Monday. Maybe she would never see him again. Bolivia was far away, a different world. In the months that he would be gone anything could happen. . . . She reached for her cup and swallowed some coffee.

'Where will you live when you get back home this summer?'

He shrugged. 'Wherever I find a position that's compatible with Martha's needs. I don't want to be gone all the time. We need to normalise our lives again.'

Normalise their lives without a wife and mother.

He still hadn't mentioned his wife, never yet told her anything about her, not even her name. The questions had been in her mind for a long time, waiting for the right moment, if ever it came, to be asked. She looked at his face, knowing she loved him, knowing too that she had to know about those many years of his past when he had loved another woman.

His eyes met hers, held them for a long, electric moment. And it seemed as if, in some strange way, he knew what she had been thinking.

'What's on your mind?' he asked softly.

Her heart was pounding with trepidation. She was afraid of doing the wrong thing, spoiling everything good between them, but she had to ask, she had to know.

Her throat was dry and she swallowed, looking at his face, his eyes. 'Lex . . . please tell me about your wife?'

CHAPTER SEVEN

Lex looked at her with an odd expression in his eyes.

'Why?'

'It seems strange not to know about her.' Andrea looked straight at him, suddenly no longer nervous. 'This last week ... I think we got to know each other better. You told me about yourself, your daughter, your work—everything, but somewhere there is that big void ... and I don't think I can ever really know you if I don't know anything about your wife and your marriage.' She was very calm. If he still didn't trust her, then nothing else mattered.

'Is that why you told me about your husband?'

'Yes.' She hesitated. 'I wanted you to understand about me, about Bart and me. He was part of my life and I can never just forget that.' She looked at him, not wavering. 'Part of me will always belong to him.'

His hand clasped hers so hard it almost hurt. He didn't speak, just looked at her with a strange light in his eyes—as if he'd just made an overwhelming discovery. After a long, silent moment, he lifted her hand and came to his feet. 'Come on, let's dance,' he said huskily. He held her against him as if he was afraid she would run. The music flowed around them sensuously, languorously, and they moved around as in a dream. There was nothing better in the world than this ... a man to love and hold.

The music came to an end much too soon, and

she felt deprived standing in the silence, the dream gone.

'Let's go home,' he whispered in her ear.

The taxi ride took mere minutes. They climbed the stairs slowly, the old wooden steps creaking under their feet. Noise filtered through the old lady's door—the sound of her television set turned up too high. Her attic was like heaven, warm and cheerful and comforting. A good place to return to on a cold winter night.

Having put away their coats, Lex pulled her next to him on the couch, took her face in his hands and kissed her briefly.

'Now,' he said, 'I'll tell you about Anja.'

'Anja.' Andrea repeated the name, soft and feminine, as if to try out the sound. 'I never even knew her name,' she said. 'What did she look like?'

'Auburn hair, grey eyes, a little taller than you. She was no beauty in the standard understanding of the word, but to me she had it all. She was lively and spirited, always happy and laughing, or so I remember her. There were other times when she wasn't like that, but I don't remember them so well.' He seemed lost in memory for a moment, saying nothing. He took her hand and held it very tightly, looking directly at her. 'I loved her,' he said softly. 'I loved her madly.'

And then the words came tumbling out, sentences, short and long and full of feeling. And it seemed as if all of what he was telling her now had been waiting to be said and expressed, waiting for the right time, the right moment.

Andrea did not interrupt, asked no questions. Sitting very quietly next to him, she took in the words and their meaning, forming in her mind a picture of the vivacious, redhaired woman who had been his wife, who was the mother of his daughter, that beautiful girl she had seen in the picture with her bright eyes and sparkling face.

'The first few months of her pregnancy,' he said, 'she was sick every day, from morning to night. She couldn't keep any food down. Pills didn't help. I felt as if it was all my fault, as if I'd made her so miserable. I'd done this to her.' He smiled. 'Here I was, with all my education and all my capacity for reasoned thought, and I was reduced to nothing but emotion—guilt and anger at her misery. Thank God, it passed, and she started eating and growing like a damned balloon.' He laughed again. 'She was beautiful.'

He was still holding her hand and after a while he looked up and his lips quirked into a smile. 'You really want to hear all that, Andrea? You want to sit here with me, listening to me talk about my wife?'

She nodded, her eyes in his. 'Yes, I do.' Her voice was low. Strange emotions were churning away inside her. Emotions she didn't quite understand. She, Andrea, was in love with this man, and here she was listening to him talk about his love for another woman. In a strange way it hurt her, and it made no sense. An ache, a longing. *Love me too! Love me as you loved her!* The words echoed in her heart, but she could not speak them out loud. She couldn't ask for love; it had to be given freely.

Lex continued then, talking about the birth of his daughter, the years that followed, the life in Bolivia. Memories—happy ones, sad ones, funny ones—all blending together into a dancing, whirling image of joy and love.

'She had this habit of walking around the house

with a glass of soda water. She'd drink the stuff from
a wine glass and she'd have it any time of the day
from morning to night. She'd leave the glasses everywhere—I'd find them in the bathroom, the bedroom,
in the car. It used to drive me wild and she'd only
laugh. We couldn't even buy the stuff locally. We
had to cart it back from La Paz by the car load.' He
looked at Andrea, a sad half-smile suddenly crossing
his face. 'After she died,' he said in a low tone, 'there
were no more glasses scattered through the house.
And then I wanted them, I wanted to find them, to
see them, to know she was still alive.'

Andrea swallowed and looked away. Tears were
pressing behind her eyes and she blinked them away
furiously. Why was she reacting this way? Why was
she subjecting herself to listening to the story of the
love he had once had, and lost?

She stood up and walked to the kitchen. She ran
the tap and had a glass of water. Her hand was
trembling. Taking a deep breath, she walked back
into the living room. He was sitting where she had
left him, head leaning back, eyes closed. She sat
down next to him again and he opened his eyes. He
searched her face for a long moment, but made no
comment.

Andrea lowered her glance to her hands in her
lap, licking dry lips. 'You haven't told me how she
died.'

'An accident. She used to take long walks—she
had so much energy all the time. Even at that altitude she didn't slow down much. There are nothing
but rough trails where I live, hugging the mountains,
with very steep slopes on the sides. She must have
tripped and fallen down.' His voice was very calm,
almost businesslike. 'We found her the next day. Her

neck and back were broken and she must have died instantly.'

'Oh, God!' The shock of it overwhelmed her. 'Oh, God!' she whispered. 'How horrible!'

Lex looked at her sideways, his eyes suddenly blank and dead again. 'Yes, like a nightmare. I kept telling myself it was too gruesome to be true, too gruesome to have happened for real. I didn't want to believe it.'

'And it was just an accident? It sounds almost as if somebody might have pushed her.'

'Yes, I know, I kept thinking that, too.' There was a bitter twist around his mouth now. 'I almost *wanted* it to be that way, just so I had a way to vent my anger, to retaliate. I wanted to blame somebody, I wanted somebody to be responsible so I could get my hands on him and strangle him.' He let out a deep sigh. 'Only there was no reason, no reason whatever to believe there was any foul play involved. No reason and no evidence. The police checked it out, as much as they were able to, and I myself racked my brain for some kind of explanation. There was none. It was an accident, pure and simple.'

He stood up, moving restlessly across the room, coming to a halt in front of the Monet reproduction on the wall. He gazed at it in silence, but Andrea knew he was seeing nothing of the picture, the colour, the detail, that the images playing through his mind had nothing to do with the calm serenity of the painting.

She came over to where he stood and lightly touched his arm. 'Thank you for telling me.'

A brief smile curved his mouth and slowly, thoughtfully, he shook his head.

'No, I thank you. Thank you for listening. I don't

know any other woman who'd have been willing to
do that.'

Andrea was silent, knowing nothing to say to
that.

'I realise now,' he went on, 'how much I needed
to talk about her, about our life together. And you're
so very right—there will always be a part of me that
will belong to her. And you understand that, and
I'm so very glad you do.' He moved suddenly, taking
her into his arms, holding her tightly against him.
'Andrea,' he said unsteadily, 'oh, Andrea. . . .' His
voice broke and nothing more came. She felt the
tense, rigid control of his body as she stood against
him and all she could do was to hold him. Slowly
she felt him relax. Finally he stepped back and raked
his hand through his hair.

'You look very tired,' he said softly. 'You should
have been in bed hours ago. Some doctor I am!'

He was right—she was exhausted, both physically
and emotionally. She gave a deep sigh. 'Yes, I'd
better go to bed now.'

He kissed her lightly. 'Sleep well.'

'*Welterusten.*'

Andrea lay in the dark, listening to his movements
in the next room, her mind full of all he had revealed
to her about his wife and the marriage they had had
together. From the way he had talked about his wife
and from the pain in his eyes she knew that he had
not yet accepted her death fully. He still missed her;
he still longed for her.

Impatiently she wiped a hand across her face. Her
cheeks were wet. She, Andrea, loved him now, but
not until he had learned to be at peace with his past,
was there any hope for her. Whatever his feelings
were for her, they certainly didn't match the deep

love and passion he had once felt for his wife.

Lex needed to do some shopping the next day—shirts and shoes to take back with him to Bolivia.

'Would you please come along?' he asked. 'I can use some advice.'

'Men's clothing is not my department.'

His eyebrows quirked up. 'No? Tell me you never bought clothes for that husband of yours.'

'Never—I was his wife, not his mother. He was perfectly capable of buying his own clothes.'

'Not many wives consider their husbands capable of choosing their own things. He must have been really something, that man of yours.' His tone was light.

Andrea smiled, looking directly at him. 'He was. He had a great taste in clothes, for one thing.'

'Excellent taste in women too.'

'Of course. He picked me.'

'Confident, aren't you?' There were laughing lights in his eyes.

She nodded smugly. 'Yep.'

A question formed in the back of her mind. Would he ever be able to talk about Anja in this light and easy way? Would he be able to mention her name and refer to her without the pain so clearly in his eyes as she had seen it yesterday? It had taken time for her. It would take time for him too, but already there was such a change in him. He was going to be all right. *He was going to be all right!*

It was a perfect day, cold, crisp and sunny, and the city was full of people doing their shopping or just strolling along looking at the window displays. A street-organ cranked out popular tunes. On the Dam a group of Hare Krishnas chanted a monotonous melody accompanied by the clanging of their cymbals.

The day went by with a lighthearted joy that made Andrea's heart sing. She felt wonderful, wanting to skip along the pavement, dance in the street. She felt seventeen again. And Lex was happy too, she could tell by his goodnatured amusement of her, the easy laughter, and the way he reached for her hand so many times during the day.

He kissed her until she was breathless after they came home that night, and she clung to him, the elation of the day soaring higher now she was in his arms. Oh, she loved him, she wanted him, and there was only one way this day could end. . . .

Only it didn't. Her happy mood shattered as Lex stepped back from her. He was breathing hard and she noticed his hands clenched by his sides. She took a shaky step forward, but he stopped her from coming closer by an almost indiscernible shaking of his head.

Her heart made a sickening lurch and she sank down in the nearest chair. There was nothing she could think of to say, nothing she even wanted to say.

'Andrea. . . .' His voice was very low. 'It was a beautiful, perfect day. I don't want you to be sorry about the way it ended, not tomorrow, not ever.'

'*Sorry?* How can you say that? How could I ever be sorry?'

'I don't know.' His voice was toneless now. 'Maybe *I* would be sorry—for taking advantage of that generous heart of yours, for leaving you again, all alone in this small attic, knowing how much you need a man to love you, and all I'd do is spend the night with you and fly off again into the blue yonder.'

There was a lump in her throat and she swallowed at it desperately. He was thinking about her, worrying about her.

'I can take care of myself, Lex. You don't need to worry about me.'

'No? Shouldn't I? Should I just care about myself, about what I want, what I feel? The day after tomorrow I'm going to leave you, and I want to make it as easy as possible for both of us.'

Andrea had no answer. She bent her head and covered her face with her hands. Why, oh, why did it have to be this way? So many years alone . . . and finally she had found someone to love—and he was leaving her.

'Stand up, Andrea.' He pulled her to her feet. She looked up to meet his eyes, seeing the sadness that matched her own. He released her hand and he was not touching her at all now. 'Please,' he said softly. 'Please go to bed now.'

Their last day together. The knowledge of it overshadowed everything, dulled the perfection of the moments they shared, the laughter and the joy of their being together. And Lex felt it too, it was in his eyes, in the way he looked at her, the way he spoke.

The last time, Andrea thought as they climbed the gloomy stairs late that night. *The last time.* The words echoed in her mind over and over.

He opened the door and let her in ahead of him, switching on the light. Having disposed of their coats he produced a bottle of Burgundy and poured each of them a glass. Andrea sat down in the rattan chair and Lex lowered himself on to the couch, patting the seat next to him. 'Sit over here,' he commanded.

She rose and did as he had asked. His arm came around her and his fingers began to play with her hair. 'You're quiet,' he commented. 'You haven't said a word since we got in that taxi.'

'I don't know what to say,' she muttered miserably.

'Well, I do. First of all, I'm glad I came. I got to know you better. Secondly, I'd like us to make a date for this summer. I'd like very much to come back and see you again.'

It took all her strength to smile at him. 'Yes, I'd like that too.'

'It's a deal. *Afgesproken*.' He got up, moved over to the stereo and selected a record.

A burst of sound flooded the room—*Rise*, by Herb Alpert, lively, rhythmic, overwhelming. Surprise was her first reaction, then anger took over. She got to her feet so hastily, wine spilled from her glass.

'I don't want to listen to that!' Her voice shook and she glared at him in anger. 'I'm not in the mood for that!'

'I know you're not.' Lex's voice was very calm. 'And neither am I, for that matter.'

'Take it off, please.'

'No.' He looked dark and alien, suddenly, and a tight knot of misery grew inside her.

'Lex,' she said slowly, 'you don't need to give me a way out. You're not responsible for me.'

He looked at her, eyes unreadable. His hand reached out and turned down the volume. She came towards him and he drew her against him.

'Andrea,' he said unevenly, 'I know you can take care of yourself; you've done it a long time. But please, let me do it tonight. I want to take care of both of us.' A slight pause. 'You're going to your bed, and I'm going to mine.'

It took a moment before she felt composed enough to speak.

'All right.' By some miracle her voice sounded calm. She moved out of his arms, not looking at him. Picking up the empty wine glasses and the bottle, she carried them to the kitchen. She felt nothing; she wasn't going to. She turned on the hot water tap full force and washed the glasses with too much soap and too much energy. She put them away and walked back into the room. Lex was leaning back in the chair, eyes closed.

'I'm going to bed now,' she said. '*Welterusten*.'

He looked at her then. 'Goodnight, Andrea.'

She walked past his chair and his hand reached out and pulled her on to his lap. He kissed her hard, almost violently, then released her. He said nothing. Without a word of her own, she went into her room, then to the bathroom to get ready for bed.

He had turned up the volume again and the music marched through the attic. She felt like screaming.

She lay in bed, listening, and it seemed to go on for ever and ever, louder and wilder until she turned over and buried her face in the pillow, covering her ears with her hands.

He didn't want to make love to her.

Damn him!

He was here, right outside her door, and still she was alone in bed. She could have wept with utter desolation, but she wouldn't let herself.

The music came to an end, abruptly, and the silence was total. Then she heard Lex move around, into his room and out again, and she lay very still, listening. Later he came back into his room. She heard his chair move, then silence. He was in bed.

Half an hour later she was still awake, the silence

screaming in her ears. She was still lying on her stomach, her hands clenched beside her face.

There was a sudden movement in the next room. She held her breath. A soft knock on the door. She didn't answer. The door opened slowly and she saw Lex's dark silhouette advance towards her. She closed her eyes and turned her face back into the pillow. He sat down on the edge of the bed.

'Andrea, are you awake?'

'Yes.' Her voice was muffled by the pillow.

His hand came down on her hair. 'I'm sorry,' he said gently.

'For what?'

'For hurting you.'

'I'm not hurt.' It was a blatant lie.

He was silent for a moment. 'Andrea, I want you . . . very much. Ever since I came back.' He was stroking her hair, then pushed it aside. 'Sit up,' he said softly.

She did so, her heart hammering loudly. In the dark her eyes searched his face. 'Why don't you want to sleep with me?'

'I want to. I want to so very much I'm going crazy. But I've tried to explain my saner arguments against it, and there's also the fact that you're so damned young, twenty-four, and here I am, thirty-six. Sometimes I wonder what the hell I'm thinking of at all.'

Andrea gave an incredulous laugh. 'I can't believe you're saying that! Our whole relationship, the talks we've had, the things we've done together—it never mattered. Never mattered at all.'

'I know.'

'You talk as if—as if I'm some seventeen-year-old virgin!'

Lex laughed. 'That, I suppose, you're not. Only sometimes you seem so young and innocent. You believe in all that's right and good. You're so straightforward and honest and so goddamned vulnerable. I don't want to hurt you. You've been hurt enough.'

'I'm a grown woman, Lex—you know that. You're not responsible for me.'

He smiled ruefully. 'I'm responsible for my own actions. You can't just interfere in other people's lives without taking responsibility.'

It was silent for a while. Andrea looked down on the blanket, feeling a strange wonderment fill her. Lying in bed earlier, she had felt rejected. And all that time he had only thought of her, placing her feelings ahead of his own.

'Andrea?' He lifted her chin, looked at her. 'You've given me so much, so much more than you can possibly know. I don't want to walk out of here tomorrow feeling I've taken one thing too many.'

Tears pricked behind her eyes. 'You never made demands. You would only take what was given freely.'

'Oh, God, Andrea,' he groaned, pulling her to him, 'I'm going out of my mind thinking about you!' He held her so tight she could barely breathe. Lex relaxed his hold on her a moment later and looked down into her eyes with so much longing, a small shiver of excitement ran down her spine.

He let out a deep sigh. 'This is the strangest situation I've ever found myself in with a woman.'

'Yes,' she said softly. 'I don't imagine you ever tried to talk yourself out of making love to someone you wanted to sleep with.'

'You're not just someone to sleep with.'

She lowered her glance, saying nothing, and the silence around them was alive with intangible vibrations.

'Andrea, am I crazy?' he said then—softly, so softly.

She looked at him, at his face, shadowed in the darkness. 'Yes,' she whispered. 'Yes, you are. You wouldn't hurt me, don't you know?'

'Kiss me,' he said unsteadily, 'kiss me.'

She did, freeing all her pent-up emotions, showing him all she felt for him, and he responded with a hungry demand that thrilled her senses.

'Don't leave me,' she murmured. 'Please stay with me.'

Lex didn't answer. He was beyond talking now, his hands moving over her body in intimate exploration. There was nothing now but the two of them and the wondrous mutual excitement that enveloped them, overwhelmed them, consumed them—an instinctive force sweeping them away irresistibly. It was an urgent, wordless lovemaking and they clung to each other with mindless, helpless intensity.

Afterwards Lex still held on to her, his arms and legs enfolding her in a gesture of intimate possession. They lay together in the narrow bed, still not speaking, and after a while he slowly began to kiss her face, her eyes in long, lingering kisses.

'Oh, Andrea,' he whispered, 'oh, Andrea, some woman you are!'

It was good. It was right between them. She hadn't felt so utterly happy for a long, long time. A powerful emotion washed over her, a giddy relief that brought tears to her eyes. And then, inexplicably, she was crying.

His body grew still against hers. 'You're crying,' he said incredulously. 'Oh, God, Andrea, I'm sorry.' He hugged her convulsively. 'Don't cry, please don't cry.'

'I'm all right,' she said, squeezing the words out between sobs. She tried to stop the tears, but it took a long time before they subsided. Weak and exhausted, she lay against him.

'Tell me, Andrea, please tell me what's wrong.' His voice was very gentle, his hands holding her firmly against him.

'Nothing's wrong,' she answered shakily. 'It's just that . . . that. . . .'

'What?'

She hid her face against his shoulder. 'I . . . I was beginning to think there was something wrong with me.'

There was a momentary silence, then his hands took her face between them, forcing her to look at him. He smiled into her eyes.

'Nothing is wrong with you, absolutely nothing. Why would you think that?'

'I haven't . . . slept with anyone in the last few years. I couldn't, I just couldn't.' Her words were barely audible.

She hadn't been interested. She'd felt no love, no passion, not even physical desire for any of the men who had entered her life. It seemed she had not been capable of feeling anything more than mild interest or low-key friendship. Bart's memory had entered every relationship she had had. Fair or unfair, no one had ever measured up. No one but Lex.

His eyes searched her face in silence.

'Why?' he asked after a pause.

'I never wanted to. Something always got in the way.'

'Memories?'

'Yes.'

'And tonight?'

'No memories.' She hesitated for a moment. 'I wanted you,' she added softly. 'Only you.'

'Oh, Andrea!' He kissed her very gently. 'It was the same for me,' he said softly, 'and it was wonderful, more wonderful than I can ever tell.'

Warm, sweet sensation woke her in the middle of the night, and she half-opened her eyes, seeing moonlight filtering faintly through the curtains. She let out a deep sigh of contentment and closed her eyes again. Something was happening to her, something altogether wonderful and special. Her mind was fuzzy with sleep and awareness came to her slowly—the warmth of Lex's body wrapped around hers in the narrow bed, his hand stroking her with slow, sensuous movements. For a few moments she lay very still, absorbing the languorous delight of his caresses. Then she stirred, making a soft, involuntary sound. He began to kiss her and again there were no words, only the feelings and sensations of their bodies. It was good and natural and full of tenderness and love. And fulfilling, utterly fulfilling.

She slept again. When she woke up, Lex was gone. Alone in the bed, she felt bereft and forlorn. She had wanted him there, next to her. She wanted him there for the rest of her life—next to her in bed, next to her in love and life.

But today he would leave her.

He would go back to Apeldoorn to see his daughter and in a few days he would be on a plane back to South America. It would be months before he would be back in the country and anything could happen. Maybe she would never see him again.

The thought alone was like a pain. Andrea huddled under the covers and shut her eyes tightly, as if by closing out her surroundings she could close out reality. A sound made her open her eyes.

Lex stood by the bed, holding a cup of tea. 'You finally woke up. *Goeiemorgen.*'

Andrea struggled up in bed, tucking the sheet around her. '*Goeiemorgen.*' She reached for the cup and smiled. 'You spoil me.'

'You deserve it.' There was warmth in his eyes, awareness of their night together, and suddenly, ridiculously, she felt acutely embarrassed. Blood rushed into her cheeks and he gave a shout of laughter.

'Oh, no,' he said, 'don't go shy on me now!'

She almost choked on her tea. 'Don't make fun of me! Don't laugh at me!'

'But I'm enjoying it. I like seeing you ruffled and off balance. With you that's not so easily accomplished.' He sat down on the side of the bed and leaned forward, his face very close, the laughter gone. 'How are you?' he asked softly.

She looked into his eyes. 'Fine.' Her voice sounded strange.

'No regrets?'

Andrea shook her head, not trusting her voice. How could she ever be sorry for loving him?

Lex straightened and watched her finish her tea, then took the cup from her and put it down. His face was very grave.

'Andrea, before I go today, there are some things that need to be said.'

She looked at him in mild surprise. 'Yes?'

He took her hands. 'About last night—I want to thank you for trusting me, for being so honest and straightforward about your feelings. It's one of the greatest gifts people can give each other—trust, sincerity.' There was tenderness in his eyes as he looked at her. Faint colour crept in her cheeks and her heart filled with warm emotion.

His fingers tightened around hers. 'We talked about responsibility, remember? Well, I realise that we took some risk last night, and I don't take that lightly. And it was not only your responsibility, it was also mine.' He paused, searching her face. 'Andrea,' he said softly, 'if you find you're pregnant, I want to know about it.'

It was impossible to utter a sound. She looked down at their hands locked together. He's thinking about me, she thought as love and gratitude flooded through her. He cares about me, about what happens to me.

'Promise me, Andrea. Promise me you'll let me know.'

She looked up into his eyes and something thrilled between them.

'I will,' she said quietly. 'I promise I will.'

'And please,' he said then, 'please promise me that if you're pregnant you won't do anything drastic.' His eyes held hers locked with strange intensity and she could feel herself begin to tremble.

'Why?' Her voice was a mere breath of sound.

'Because,' he said slowly, 'life is too precious.'

Tears welled up in her eyes and she blinked them away. 'Thank you,' she whispered.

Lex smiled a slow, gentle smile, took her in his arms and held her close. 'Thank you for what?'

'For caring.'

'Oh, Andrea. . . . I care. I care very much.'

For a long time they silently held each other close until he quietly put her from him.

'And now you can get dressed while I get breakfast, and after that you can go to work.'

She looked at him in surprise. 'Go to work? But you're leaving today. I can go tomorrow.'

'It would be better, I think, if you'd go today. Then I wouldn't have to leave you behind alone in the apartment. If I just leave the place empty it wouldn't seem so much of a goodbye.' He smiled as he spoke the words, as if mildly mocking his own sentimentality.

Andrea was grateful for his suggestion, because she, too, did not like goodbyes, and going to work would take care of the rest of the day. She wondered if that, too, had been on his mind—the fact that otherwise she would have been alone for the rest of the day.

So she left him at the door after he had kissed her hard and quickly, saying he would come back in July. And hastily she turned and ran down the stairs while tears threatened to overwhelm her.

Then she was in the street, with icy rain lashing her face. She ran around the corner to the tram stop, and luckily she didn't have to wait too long.

The day passed in a rush of activity. So much to do, so many things to organise, stacks of applications to read through. She could take some of them home to read tonight, but by the time it was five she was exhausted and all she wanted to do was go home and crawl into bed. It was obvious that she didn't have all her strength back, and it annoyed her.

She dragged herself home, climbed the stairs and

stood in front of her door, breathless. Nobody would be there to welcome her. Lex was gone. Sylvia was gone. She opened the door and went inside. The place was empty and silent. Lex's room—or rather Sylvia's room—was immaculate. Not a sign that he had been there for a week and a half. Loneliness swept over her as her eyes surveyed the vacant room.

Alone again, she thought. The story of my life. I can't stand this any more. She wanted to cry, but wouldn't let herself. She'd manage. She'd done it many times and she could do it again. Softly she closed the door.

As she went into the kitchen her eyes caught a splash of colour on the table. Her heart lurched and warmth flooded her.

Lex had left something behind after all.

CHAPTER EIGHT

A RED rose. A beautiful, long-stemmed red rose in a slender glass bud vase. A note lay on the table in front of it. 'Dear Andrea,' she read, 'don't forget, I'll be back in July.' Her eyes misted over, but her sense of desolation softened a little. He would come back. It wasn't all so bad, because this time he had not said goodbye. This time she had the gift of hope.

But January to July was a long time, and sometimes it seemed interminable. It was not easy, this waiting, and for a while after Lex had left it was difficult to adjust to being alone again. The attic seemed dreary with his absence. She thought about her feelings for him, analysed them, dissected them, put them back in order again. But all that resulted was the same bit of truth—the fact that she loved him and that she was lonely, bitterly lonely. She had shared herself in every possible way with a man who was no longer within her reach and all that she had left were the memories and the waiting for his return.

At the end of January Sylvia came back with a winter tan and a new collection of stories, and life took on its normal routine. Andrea was grateful for Sylvia's presence, it made her feel less alone.

She was not pregnant. She had not really expected to be, although, strangely, the possibility had held no terror for her. She had thought about it after Lex had left, wondering what if . . . and she had concluded that somehow she would manage.

She wrote Lex a letter. It was awkward writing
him, because she didn't like writing letters very much
and putting words on paper seemed such a final,
definite thing to do. He had promised to return, but
telling him she was not expecting a baby almost
seemed like cutting strings, giving him back his freedom. And somehow it hurt, even though she had
never demanded his attachment to her, or his obligation. On the contrary, she had made sure he
understood that she felt responsible for her own life
and her own decisions.

He answered her letter and she sensed he too did
not like writing letters very much. He wrote that he
was glad she was well, that time for him seemed to
pass slowly, but that he was working hard. He told
her a little about what he was doing, but not very
much, and all in all it seemed like a letter from a
stranger to a stranger. She put down a sudden urge
to cry.

We are *not* strangers, she told herself fiercely. We
just don't know how to write letters, how to put the
words together to convey what we really want to
say. Maybe it's better, she thought, maybe it's better
not to say too much too soon.

She put the letter away and did not read it again.
Instead she remembered the rose every time she
thought of him.

Twice she tried writing another letter, tearing
them up both times. There was an aching need inside
her to keep some kind of contact, just so Lex
wouldn't seem so totally out of reach. But it seemed
that what she wanted to tell him she couldn't write,
and what she could write didn't matter. She didn't
want to overwhelm him with her feelings, not expressed on paper anyway. So finally she wrote him a

note with nothing more than a few meaningless paragraphs about Sylvia's return, her job, the weather. She couldn't imagine why he would care about the ice and snow, but it was something to say.

One night, endless weeks later, she found an airmail letter from him on the coffee table. She picked it up with a hand that suddenly trembled, and ripped the envelope open with shaky fingers. For the last weeks she had come home every night hoping there would be a letter from him, and now here it was.

It was a friendly letter, but a little awkward. It was obvious that he was used to the more formal and objective style of scientific writing. He didn't tell her much about his feelings and thoughts, but then she hadn't either.

The letter disappointed her, as she had been afraid it would, and hoped it wouldn't. Her stomach contracted as if in pain. It all seemed so hopeless, so futile.

A moment later Sylvia came out of her room, gave a cheerful hello and announced that she'd get dinner tonight—*hutspot*, if that was all right with Andrea. To go with it there were meatballs left from yesterday that only needed reheating.

Hutspot was fine with Andrea. It was one of the few dishes Sylvia knew how to prepare half-way decently. Anything that required more talent than boiling potatoes, carrots and onions in one pan and then mashing them up together was beyond her expertise.

'How's Alexander the Great doing?' Sylvia enquired as they were eating. Her tone was casual, the question asked between two bites of food.

Alexander the Great. On an earlier occasion Sylvia had called him 'a great hunk of man'. Andrea felt immensely irritated at the stupidity of those labels. They had nothing to do with the real man she knew, and she had never thought of him in those terms. She thought of him in many different ways, memories alive of the loneliness in his eyes, the bitter anguish the time she had held him in her arms when he had finally broken down. Memories, too, of this past January when he had been so different, so full of caring and loving for her. . . .

'Did I say something wrong?' Sylvia looked surprised, blue eyes wide and innocent.

'Where did you get that stupid name?'

Sylvia shrugged. 'His sisters started it. He was quite a loverboy when he was young—lots of girls hanging around him all the time, or so they tell me— it was before my time, you know. Anyway, the name stuck.' She continued eating and didn't mention Lex again.

The dishes done, Sylvia left to see a friend and Andrea settled down to work on her bedspread. It was coming along nicely, bright and colourful, just the way she wanted it. It would cheer up her room. Only it would be covering a single bed. It would look more cheerful if it would be bigger, covering a double.

Lex was in her thoughts all the time. Her memory was filled with things he had said and done—little bits of conversation or just a single phrase would pop up at the most unlikely times. '. . . the little monster himself reminded me of myself.' '. . . you need me.' 'I loved her. I loved her madly.' 'Oh, Andrea, some woman you are!' 'He must have been really something, that man of yours.' Even in memory she could clearly see his face, hear his voice.

Did he love her?

Did he love her enough? Enough to put his past behind him and make a new beginning?

She stared idly at the little square of orange material in her hand. Hundreds of tiny flowers in brilliant colours danced in front of her eyes, like the sparks of hope dancing through her mind.

April and May brought better weather. Sunshine, blue skies. Daffodils, tulips and hyacinths bloomed in profusion all over the city—in the parks, public gardens and flower beds. Amsterdam was gearing up again for the tourist season and foreigners were already appearing in greater numbers.

Time for spring cleaning. Andrea made a half-hearted attempt at it, glad her mother wasn't there to see her feeble efforts. The place wasn't dirty anyway, so why all the exertion? Tradition, that's why, she told herself. Tradition and custom were responsible for many evils in this world, she decided grimly.

She was bored, living from day to day without much enthusiasm for anything. A tour around the country to do interviews with candidates for a year of study overseas alleviated the problem a little. At least it was a break in the monotony of her everyday routine.

Soon after that Sylvia packed up and left for home before going on a tour guiding assignment to Venice. Being alone again seemed not so bad now because July was not far off.

Soon Lex will be back. It was a thought that repeated itself almost automatically. She felt better than she had for months. Her vacation was scheduled for July and Annette had agreed not to put down the exact dates yet.

And then a letter from Lex arrived. With nervous fingers Andrea tore open the envelope and began to read the words on the flimsy airmail paper.

He wasn't coming back. Not in July.

Her heart sank and tears of anger and disapointment filled her eyes. She couldn't read and her fingers held on so tightly to the paper, it crumpled. Damn him! she thought wildly. Damn him for doing this to me!

Slowly she took a deep breath, forcing back the tears. She wasn't going to cry, not if it killed her!

Smoothing the paper, she read on. Unexpected complications, he wrote. Trouble with one of the contracts, interfering bureaucrats. Etcetera, etcetera. It would take at least another six, maybe eight weeks to straighten it all out. He wouldn't be able to leave until the middle of September.

September!

Her whole body was tight with the effort not to cry, or scream, or throw something.

I can't take this, she thought. *I can't take this endless waiting!*

Curling up into a corner of the couch, she lowered her head on to her pulled-up knees and squeezed her eyes shut. For a long time she just sat there until finally there was nothing but a numbness inside her.

A card from Sylvia came a few days later, one of your typical tourist cards with your typical gondola in one of your typical Venice canals.

'The canals are dirty,' she wrote in tiny scribbles, 'but then so are ours, so who am I to complain?

Having a good time. Nice bunch of people. Lex's daughter is going to Bolivia for the summer. Heard through the family grapevine that he's chasing the women again—hope so! *Groetjes*, Sylvia. P.S. You didn't fall for him, I hope?'

Andrea tore up the card in tiny pieces, feeling sick. Her stomach felt so tight it hurt. Taking a cardigan off the chair, she swung out of the door, ran down the stairs, out into the street. No thinking now, no feeling. Just walking, doing something, going somewhere. Turning the corner, she almost bumped into Pieter.

He gave her a wide grin. 'I'm glad you're ready. Let's go.'

She stared at him, saying nothing.

'What's the matter?'

She shook her head. 'Nothing.'

'Of course not,' he said smoothly. 'Where are you going?'

'I don't know ... nowhere.'

'Good. I'm on my way there now.'

She started walking, face down, and Pieter matched his pace to hers. After a while she looked up at him.

'Were you coming to see me?'

He nodded, studying her face. 'You look like hell. Let's have a drink some place.'

Most of all she wanted to be alone, walk, just walk until she got tired and numb. Then she wanted to go to sleep. But it wasn't even six yet. It was better all the way around to go with Pieter and have that drink. Or two, or three.

'Thanks, I'd like that.'

Somehow he made her laugh that evening—over drinks, over a bad Chinese dinner, and later as they walked the long way back home. Exhausted, Andrea fell asleep almost instantly.

The phone rang while she was eating breakfast the next morning. It was Pieter.

'How are you doing?'

'Fine,' she answered, surprise in her voice.

'Good. I was just checking. Keep up the spirit, kid.'

'Yes, thank you.' She wasn't sure what else to say.

'See you around. Bye-bye.' He hung up.

Slowly she replaced the receiver. A very short conversation for sure, but she felt warmed by his concern.

He came to see her now and then after that. He was staying in Amsterdam for the summer, spending most of his time in pubs and market places to study Amsterdam humour, so he said. He visited her in her apartment and sat for hours telling her jokes and silly anecdotes. He made her laugh. It felt so good to laugh.

'It's people like you who make me feel it's all worthwhile,' he said one evening. His tone of voice made her look up into his face and she saw no laughter in his eyes. She had never really seen Pieter serious.

'What do you mean?' she asked.

'It's easy to laugh when you're happy,' he said slowly. 'But not everybody is. When I'm with you and I make you laugh and I see the spark in your eyes and the glow on your face, I'm happy. It makes me feel good about myself, about what I'm trying to do with my life. A lot of people don't take me seriously. Making silly jokes and puns and wisecracks doesn't seem like much of a job. But you see, telling the jokes isn't the job. The real job is to entertain people, to make them laugh and forget their worries, if only for a short time.'

And that was exactly what Pieter was doing to her, she realised.

'You're much too serious a girl,' he told her. 'At the moment you're my greatest challenge in life.'

But the challenge was for her laugh, not for her love. Never once did he make a pass or any kind of advance, which was a relief to Andrea. More complications in her life was not what she needed right now. Pieter treated her with the kindly affection of a brother, not treading where he was not wanted. It was as if somehow he sensed she was dying inside with the lonely waiting for another man.

So Lex was chasing the women again. '*I hope so,*' Sylvia had written. Andrea wondered to what extent this bit of news had been exaggerated. Her rational mind told her it would be good for him to be around other women again, one more step in the healing process, wasn't it? Hadn't she done the same thing— gone out with other men when finally she had had enough courage to do so?

She was dusting the bookshelves with furious energy. The card had bothered her. She felt scared and threatened, and angered by the fact that she was too far away to do anything about anything. What if he found another woman? What if he changed his mind and didn't come to Amsterdam to see her again?

She crossed to the open window and shook out the dusting cloth with an over-abundance of energy. January to September was a very long time. People changed. Feelings changed. Life changed. And she didn't even know if Lex had ever loved her. It had been too soon for that. It would be unfair to expect anything from him. And she hadn't, not really, and she'd tried to make sure he had known that. She didn't want his gratitude, or his sense of obligation. She didn't want him to love her for the wrong reasons. So there was only the waiting until he was free of his past, free of his grief. Until he was a whole man again.

Leaning out of the window, she looked down into the street below. A beautiful Saturday morning. On the other side of the street children were playing hopscotch on the pavement. Two teenage boys in jeans were dismantling a motorcycle. A young woman gingerly pushed her baby carriage past them with barely enough room to spare.

Andrea shivered. They had the sun, but she was on the shady side of the street and suddenly she felt very cold.

Her fear and uncertainty grew worse by the day. It ate away at her self-confidence, her mental strength. At night she had trouble falling asleep, worry keeping her awake. Why had she even begun to hope there might be a future for the two of them together? Lex liked her. He might even love her in some limited way, a love grown out of gratitude, appreciation, guilt or whatever, but nothing that would last. Nothing that went as deep as the love he had felt for his wife.

She took a deep breath and clenched her fists. In the long run he would get bored with her. He would need someone more outgoing and vivacious. She was nothing like that vibrant, sparkling woman his wife had been. She, Andrea, was the total opposite. Quiet, introspective. A book reader, a homebody.

Dull.

She held her breath, shocked by the word, but her mind kept repeating it—once, twice. Dull. *Dull!*.

Then anger flared, flooded her being. This was crazy! Had she gone so far as to lose her belief in herself, her self-confidence? She was *not* dull! Nobody had ever accused her of that. Bart had loved her the way she was and he could have had his pick out of a dozen smart, attractive girls, yet he had chosen her.

Something was happening to her, and she didn't like it.

She was tired. A vacation was what she needed—a few weeks on a beach in Spain or Italy, with a smooth Latin lover charming her with flowery compliments and nursing her shrivelling ego back into health. Only that sort of thing was not her style; she didn't have the personality for that kind of adventure. Idiot that she was, she sat in an Amsterdam attic withering away waiting and worrying.

Anyway, it was a moot point. She had cancelled her vacation for July and rescheduled it for September, much to Annette's relief. July was a busy month, full of last-minute hassles concerning the arrival of the new foreign students in August and the departure of the Dutch students for their various destinations overseas. A lot of things always seemed to go wrong, no matter how well planned and organised everything was: schedules and reservations had to be changed at the last minute; people who were counted on promptly broke legs or had to have their appendixes out.

Taking a vacation in September was definitely

better, said Annette. Andrea hoped so. She had answered Lex's letter saying she was sorry about the delays, that she had heard Martha was spending her vacation with him and hoped that she was happy. She closed saying she hoped to see him in September.

August passed and, earlier than expected, Sylvia came back, glowing with good health and good cheer.

'Hope you don't mind,' she said, 'but I'm moving out.' She laughed at Andrea's surprise. 'I found a better deal. I found the man of my dreams and I'm moving in with him.'

Recovered from her surprise, Andrea smiled. 'I'm glad for you.'

'Thanks. We'll come and see you, of course. I want you to meet him. And if you want to rent out the room again, just whistle. I know a half dozen people who'd move in tomorrow.'

In one day flat Sylvia had packed and departed. The 'man of her dreams' had collected her things during the day in a borrowed van. When Andrea came home that night she opened the door to Sylvia's room and the sight of it disheartened her. It was so empty and bare. The bed was stripped, pictures were taken off the wall and all Sylvia's books were gone.

She had been alone all summer, but knowing now that Sylvia would not be coming back at all seemed to increase her sense of loneliness. Still, she didn't like the idea of someone else moving in, someone else with different habits, different likes and dislikes. Getting to know another person took effort and tolerance and she didn't feel up to it. Somehow she would manage without the extra money.

Quietly she closed the door behind her. I wish I

didn't have to live here any more, she thought. Too many things have happened here and I'm tired. I don't like it here any more.

There was a knock on the door and she let out a deep sigh. Please, she thought wearily, don't let it be Ria. Not tonight.

Reluctantly she went to open the door.

CHAPTER NINE

Lex.

Andrea could not speak. Not a sound would come. Staring at him blindly, she held on to the door as a wave of emotion washed over her—relief and joy so intense she felt giddy.

Dark eyes looked at her intently. 'May I come in?'

'Yes,' she whispered, 'please.'

Swiftly he moved past her into the room, turning to face her. She was still holding on to the door, gazing at him as if hypnotised, taking in the big bulk of him, the dark eyes, the strong mouth, faintly smiling. Suddenly it was too much, too overwhelming.

Letting go of the door, she stumbled to her room and threw herself on the bed. Heaving sobs racked her body and there was no way she could stop herself, her emotions too overpowering to be expressed in any other way.

Lex was with her moments later, lifting her off the pillow and against his chest, holding her, just holding her. His arms around her, strong and secure, were like a haven. It was like coming home. Slowly she began to calm down. Finally he lifted her face to his and kissed her eyes, her mouth, then smiled and handed her his handkerchief.

'A very strange welcome,' he commented lightly. 'I thought you'd be happy to see me.'

Andrea gave a tremulous smile. 'I am happy, you know I am. I've never been so happy in my life.'

'So you cried.'

'I couldn't help it. I'd been so afraid, for so long.'

'Afraid?' he asked gently.

'I didn't know if you'd come back. I was afraid I'd never see you again.' It was no use hiding the truth. She'd broken down in tears and given herself away, utterly and completely.

He pushed a strand of hair back over her shoulder. 'I told you I was coming back,' he said quietly.

'I know. Only that was months ago, and time goes on and things change and . . . and feelings change. I'm realistic enough to know that.'

'But your feelings didn't change . . . did they?'

Andrea shook her head.

'Why did you never tell me? Those nice polite little letters you sent me . . . and never a word. Why didn't you tell me how you felt? That you were waiting for me?'

She lowered her eyes. 'I didn't know how, and it wouldn't have been fair. I . . .' She faltered, not quite knowing how to go on, how to explain.

'Fair?' His voice was very low. 'What do you mean? Why wouldn't it have been fair?'

'I . . . I didn't want you to think . . . I didn't want to ask anything of you. You needed time.' She looked up, meeting his eyes.

'Time for what?' There was a strange expression in his eyes and her heart began to thud.

'To sort out your life and your emotions. To get over your hurt and anger.' She swallowed nervously. 'All I could do was wait. It was the only fair thing to do.'

Lex looked at her with infinite tenderness, his hand smoothing her hair, smoothing and smoothing it. 'You are very courageous,' he said softly. 'And very generous and loving.'

'You keep saying that.'

'It's true.'

'I just didn't want you to come back because you felt any kind of . . . of . . .'

'Obligation?'

She nodded. 'I only wanted you to come if you wanted it yourself.'

'And here I am.'

'Yes.' His eyes held hers locked for a long silent moment and she felt herself grow warm. 'I gave myself away, didn't I?'

He nodded agreement. 'Part of your charm. I like knowing where I stand.' He touched her cheek. 'Don't worry about it.' He drew her closer, his mouth covering hers, and she closed her eyes. He kissed her deeply, his hands sliding up under her hair to hold her head. A warm tide of love washed over her—a longing, a need . . . It was like the dream she had had so many times in those lonely months—only this was real—his touch, his kisses, the feeling of the warm, solid strength of his body against her. No time to think or dream now . . . no time for anything but this—the sweet ecstasy of love rushing through her, suffusing her, carrying her away. . . .

'Andrea,' he murmured against her mouth, 'I thought of you, all those months and weeks and days. . . .' He drew back slightly, looked at her. 'My feelings didn't change,' he said huskily. 'That's the only reason I came back.'

She closed her eyes and leaned against him. 'I'm glad.' Silence enveloped them, a quivering, vibrating silence. Minutes passed until finally Lex took her hand and pulled her up with him from the bed, and led her out of the room.

Back in the living room everything seemed normal, as if nothing at all had happened.

'Have you had dinner yet?' he asked.

She shook her head. 'I'd just come home from work when you came. I'll fix us something to eat now, if you're hungry.'

'No, no. Let's go out, have a nice meal some place, go dancing afterwards.'

She smiled at him. 'Nice, I'd like that. I haven't been dancing for ages.' She looked around the room. 'Don't you have a suitcase? You're not going back to Apeldoorn so late at night, are you?'

He grinned. 'I left my suitcase on the landing. I didn't want to presume too much too soon. Is Sylvia back from her wanderings yet?'

Andrea caught the glint in his eyes. 'She came back yesterday and she moved out today.' She paused. 'You knew she wouldn't be here, didn't you?'

He looked innocent. 'She moved out?'

'Yes, and she told you, so stop pretending!'

He laughed. 'I saw her over the weekend when she was home in Apeldoorn.'

'Well, at least she didn't give you the keys this time! How did you get in downstairs?'

'Your friend Ria was most helpful.'

'I bet she was. She thinks you're the very epitome of manhood.'

Lex roared. 'Good, now I know where to go if you throw me out tonight.'

'She's married,' Andrea reminded him.

'That's right. How big is he?'

'Oh, go take a hike!' She turned, laughing. 'I'll change my clothes.'

Twenty minutes later they were going down the stairs.

'Let's just walk,' she said. She felt alive and full of energy. It stayed that way all through drinks and dinner. Happiness suffused her, a light shining inside her, warming her.

'Your eyes are like Christmas lights,' Lex said over coffee. 'And I was worried about seeing you again.'

'*Worried?*' For some reason she'd never thought he'd be worried. She was the one who'd done the worrying, hadn't she?

'January to September is a long time,' he said quietly. 'Who knows what might have happened. You worried about it, and so did I.'

His face was very serious. She wanted to touch him, kiss him, hold him tight. His eyes moved over her face and then he smiled.

'You should see yourself,' he said. 'Your heart's right there in your eyes.'

Warmth crept into her cheeks. 'Don't embarrass me.' He was like no other man she knew. She'd been teased or mocked before, but it had never affected her like this.

'And then those cool, calm little letters you wrote me,' he said again. 'I hardly recognised you. The first one you sent me. . . .' He paused, holding her gaze. 'I almost wondered if you were telling me the truth. For days I went around worrying you were really pregnant and didn't want me to know.'

'And then?'

'My sanity returned. You had promised me, and you'd been very honest and straightforward with me all the time. The only thing I could do was trust you.'

Andrea glanced down at her plate. He had

worried about her. He trusted her, he believed in her. . . .

He took her hand. 'Andrea, look at me.'

She did, feeling the warmth of his hand flowing through her as she met his eyes.

'You did tell me the truth, didn't you?'

'Yes. I would have told you. I promised you and you would have had the right to know.'

His eyes were warm and his hand tightened around hers. 'Thank you.' He released her hand. 'Would you like to go dancing now? Or shall we just go home?'

Her heart began to beat faster at the expression in his eyes. 'Let's go home.'

They walked back, taking their time. Strolling through Leidestraat, they glanced into the show windows of the fancy shops, seeing the luxurious displays of furs and jewels and antiques. They turned into the Keizersgracht where it was dark and mysterious at this hour of the night. Andrea would never dream of walking here at night, alone, but with Lex this place of hidden dangers, real or imagined, took on an atmosphere of romance. Crossing a bridge, they stopped to lean over the railing and look down into the dark, shiny water.

There was a thought in Andrea's mind, a question she had wanted to ask, but hadn't. It was dark now and it seemed easier. Standing next to him, looking into the canal, she couldn't see his face.

'Lex,' she began, 'what would you have done if I had been pregnant?'

He raised his head and looked at her. 'I would have come home and asked you to marry me.'

She wasn't sure if she was surprised or touched,

and for a moment she said nothing. 'You're old-fashioned,' she said then.

'Very. In some things. I take care of what's mine.'

'You think it would have worked?'

'We would have made it work,' he said calmly. 'We're both very experienced.'

'Oh?'

'In loving, happiness, being married.'

Andrea let that sink in, her eyes back on the water below.

'Would you have taken me back to Bolivia?' she asked after a pause.

'No, I. . . .'

She heard no more. *No!* She grew cold. Of course he wouldn't have taken her there! Bolivia was the place where he had lived with his wife. She swallowed miserably, realising he was talking and she hadn't heard a word.

'I'm sorry, I . . . I didn't hear what you said.'

He looked at her strangely. 'I said that under the circumstances it wouldn't have been a good place for you to be—the altitude, the weather, the adjustments you'd have to make to a new way of life. It would have been asking too much of you while you were pregnant.'

'Oh, I. . . .' She grasped for his hand, closing her eyes for a moment. She'd been wrong, so terribly wrong.

'I would have resigned and moved back home.'

She stared at him. *'Left your job?'* she whispered.

Moving away from the railing, he pulled her towards him. 'You may not believe this, but I *am* dispensable. Someone else could have finished the job for me. You'd have come first. You're more important than any job.'

'Oh, Lex. . . .' Her voice wobbled and she didn't go on. It filled her with gratitude and joy to think that he would have done that for her.

He kissed her eyes. 'Don't cry,' he whispered. 'Why do I always make you cry?'

'Because you're nice to me.'

Because I'm starved for some loving, she wanted to add. I've been so lonely for so long. It feels so good to have someone care about me, to be happy again.

He laughed softly, incredulously. 'Because I'm *nice* to you? Good God, Andrea. . . .' His voice was rough. 'Come on, let's go.'

She felt unaccountably nervous when they arrived home. Her heart was beating fast, but that was from climbing the stairs, of course. She fumbled with the keys and he took them from her, letting her in ahead of him. He closed the door behind him and handed back her keys, his eyes intent on her face.

She swallowed, smiled. 'Coffee?'

'No, nothing, thanks.'

Andrea turned away and put some Chopin on the record player with unsteady hands. Music helped; it always did—a presence in the room that filled a silence, smoothing away rough edges.

'Come sit with me,' invited Lex, and she slid down next to him on the couch and his arm came around her shoulders. 'What's that?' He pointed at the patchwork quilt folded up on the floor next to her sewing basket, the oranges, golds and yellows contrasting spots of colour in the quiet, cool green of the room.

'A bedspread. It's not finished yet.' She sighed. 'It's more work than I anticipated.' To be honest, she hadn't worked on it lately.

'Why those colours? Why not green?'

'Oh. . . .' She shrugged lightly. 'My green period's over. Time for a change.'

Their eyes met for a heart-stopping moment.

'Tell me,' Lex said then, his tone as light as hers had been, 'what is it you want out of life?'

Letting out a sigh, she smiled. 'To live happily ever after.'

The pause was only barely noticeable. 'Mmm . . . first you'll have to kiss the frog.'

She looked at him. A memory came back, clear and easy, as if it had been close to the surface, waiting to be recalled. *The little monster himself reminded me of myself.* She glanced up the bookshelf where the green ceramic frog had been sitting all those months in the same place. Then she looked back at Lex and his hand reached out and gently touched her cheek. 'Kiss me?' His voice was very low, his words more than just a question. She moved closer, sliding her arms around him, and kissed him without any hesitation or reluctance. His hands moved up, taking her face between them and looked deep into her eyes.

'What do you see?' he asked.

'A prince,' she said. 'Only you never were a frog.'

'Oh, yes. Don't you remember? Have you forgotten already?'

'Forgotten what?'

'The man I was when we first met. Certainly not a prince. You gave me courage, you made me laugh again.'

'Oh, come on,' she said selfconsciously. But she did remember those days, remembered the empty look in his eyes, his anguish when finally he had broken down. She had wanted, then, so much to help, to tell him she knew what he was going through. That it would pass, that life was still worth living. And now, a year later, he was telling her just that. And the joy of his acknowledgement warmed her. He took her hands and his eyes were full of tenderness.

'It's true,' he said softly. 'You understood, didn't you? You were the only one who really understood. And I looked at you, so young and vulnerable and yet so strong and courageous, and I knew then that I had to find a way to go on with my life as you had done. You showed me that it was possible.' He leaned forward and his hand came up and touched her hair, her cheek, her mouth. His eyes moved over her face and her heart skipped a beat at the look on his face. He let out a sigh and briefly closed his eyes. 'Andrea. . . .'

She leaned forward and put her arms tightly around him until there was no longer any room between them and she could feel the thudding of his heart against her breast. 'Lex,' she whispered, 'I'm so glad you came back.'

There was a slow, deep intake of breath. 'Yes. . . .' His mouth found hers in a soft, gentle kiss that suddenly changed and became filled with a hungry passion that sent her blood pounding through her body. She felt herself being lifted, put down again on her bed, and she clung to him, feeling nothing but sweet sensation.

It had been so long, so long . . . and she loved him so very much and she ached for him with a painful longing. She wanted him, needed him with all the despair of the endless waiting of the last months.

They were together again, the two of them . . . it

was good, so good to hold him again, to love him again. . . . He was hers and nothing was more important than that, nothing more intoxicating than the gentle touching of his hands and mouth. . . . Everything faded away with this wonderful, mutual loving that was theirs. . . .

No time, no place, no conscious thought, until something changed, she knew not what. Lex stopped kissing her and his body grew tense. An instant later she felt him trembling against her. He raised his face to look at her and his eyes were filled with so much anguish, the breath caught in her throat. For a terrifying moment she couldn't breathe, and in that one silent, shivering second dream turned into nightmare.

Andrea didn't understand what had happened, what was happening now. She didn't understand the pain in his eyes, why he was looking at her like that. A drowning fear washed over her, suffocating her. She wanted to cry out, but her voice carried no sound.

A moment later he was sitting on the edge of the bed, his hands covering his face, shaking. She stared at him, cold with shock, shivering. Struggling upright, she reached out and touched his bare back.

'Lex,' she whispered, 'Lex. . . .'

He took a deep, shuddering breath. 'I'm sorry.' His voice was an agonised whisper. He didn't look at her, he didn't touch her. Without another word he pushed himself up and staggered drunkenly from the room.

Andrea scrambled off the bed, but she was shaking so badly her legs wouldn't keep her up. She collapsed back down on top of the blankets, turned over and buried her face in the pillow. She lay there without crying, without thinking, without feeling, her body tight with tension, until finally, she grew cold and shivery. Numbly she crawled under the blankets, hugging them close around her. A thought, a knowing had edged its way into her consciousness.

Something was wrong, terribly wrong.

A tap on the half-open door woke her the next morning. She blinked against the bright sunlight streaming through the window. The curtains were open . . . clothes on the floor. . . . Oh, God. . . . In an effort to blot out the light, the memories, she pulled the covers over her face.

'Andrea?'

Taking the blankets off her face, she saw him come in. He was dressed—lightweight slacks, loafers, a green sweater. He sat down on the bed and looked at her, his face drawn and haggard.

'I wish I could tell you how badly I feel about what happened last night.'

'I don't understand what went wrong.' She could barely force the words out, the pain still raw inside her.

'I'm not sure myself.' The anguish was back in his eyes. 'I'm truly sorry.'

She looked at his face and something happened inside her, a strength filling her, pushing out the fear and hurt. Lex needed her and she loved him and she couldn't bear to see the torment in his face. Her hand found his and held it.

'It's all right,' she said softly. 'Let's just forget it.'

His relief was unmistakable. He touched her cheek. 'I don't deserve you,' he said unevenly. He got up, turned and walked out the door before another word could be spoken.

It was a good day. No memories of the previous night interfered, as if really all had been forgotten, as if the incident belonged to another time, another sphere. They roamed through the city on foot and by tram, buying Sunday provisions from small speciality stores—French cheese from Robert et Abraham Kef, bread from *bakker* Hartog (four kinds because they couldn't choose), and an assortment of nuts from a tiny little shop tucked away in a basement. They spent half an hour in a butchery on the Vijzelgracht, tasting different kinds of pâté under the careful guidance of the butcher who was in no hurry for them to make a choice. Tasting and choosing his wares was serious business and no client would walk out of his store with something that didn't totally delight him. Lex played along like a true connoisseur, and they came away with enough to last them a week.

'We'll need to buy some coffee, too,' Lex decided. 'Something very rare and exotic.'

'We may not like it,' she said.

'You're a pessimist. Do you know where to go?'

'There's a shop in Warmoesstraat, a great place— very old-fashioned, with red silos full of beans, and brass scales and. . . .'

'Just what I like, let's go.'

'I can't believe you like this sort of thing. Men are supposed to hate shopping.'

'I haven't been in Amsterdam for ages. I always miss it when I'm gone. There's no place in the whole wide world that comes close.'

Andrea laughed. 'Oh dear, the words of a true Amsterdammer!'

He stood still on the pavement and looked at her with mock seriousness. 'Tell me, is there any other city in the world that has a piggy bank museum?'

She stared at him. 'A *what*?'

'A piggy bank museum.'

'Don't tell me, there's one here.' She could barely contain her laughter.

Lex nodded gravely. 'Now you know, there's no place like Amsterdam.' He began to walk again and she followed him, laughing.

It amazed her that he was spending an entire Saturday wandering around town doing nothing more important than buying bread and meat and coffee. It was a game, it was all a game and he was enjoying it, as she was enjoying it. Laughing, holding hands, kissing in a dark corner were all part of the happiness of being together again. It filled her with gratitude to see him so radiant and lighthearted, to hear the easy laughter. And every time his eyes met hers, love flooded her like a warm tide. She loved him. She loved him so very much.

By four o'clock she was exhausted. 'I've had it. I want to go home, or sit down, or something.'

Lex looked at his watch. 'A little early for drinks. Let's have some tea. All right with you?'

'Anything is all right with me,' she said. *Anything as long as you don't leave me again*, she added silently.

He steered her deftly across the street. 'You're too easy,' he said lightly. 'Aren't you ever going to disagree or argue or fight with me?' He opened the door to a small restaurant and let them in. They found a table in a corner and a waiter came over almost immediately. It had been like that at lunch—instant service—and at all the other times she had been out with him. Nobody missed Lex Vermeer when he walked into a room, and nobody would ever let him wait.

He ordered a pot of tea. 'You want something to go with it?'

'*Appeltaart*,' she said promptly. 'With whipped cream. If I may.'

'You may.' He ordered the apple cake and the waiter departed. 'You haven't answered my question yet,' he said then.

'What question?'

'I was asking if you're never going to disagree or argue or fight with me.'

'Only if you become impossible,' she said lightly.

'You've seen me at my worst.' His voice was suddenly very quiet. 'Remember last year?'

'I don't think my getting angry at you was what you needed just then.'

He looked at her for a long moment. 'You know, sometimes I *wanted* you to get angry, but all I ever saw was calmness in those blue eyes of yours. Miss Serenity, if I ever saw one.'

Andrea shrugged selfconsciously. 'I'm a calm person. I always was.'

'Don't you ever get mad?'

'Of course I do! Why do you ask?'

He frowned. 'I don't know, I've been wondering.'

'Well, I do get angry sometimes. I've been angry, terribly angry.' She paused. 'After Bart died there were moments that I was in a rage. I was furious with life, with God, with fate ... with Bart himself for dying and leaving me.' She gave a faint smile.

'Don't worry, I know how to get angry.' A memory stirred suddenly. 'Besides, you *have* seen me mad! First time you ever saw me I was so furious I wanted to strangle you barehanded.'

He laughed. 'How could I have forgotten!'

Tea and apple cake were put in front of her. She sat back lazily and enjoyed it. The cake was good, with lots of cream. By the time she'd finished it she felt as if she'd eaten a meal.

Lex was watching her with amusement. 'There goes your appetite. What about dinner?'

Guiltily Andrea looked down at her empty plate. 'I'll be hungry again, later.'

'Why don't we go home and when we get hungry we'll start on the cheese and pâté. We might as well, there's enough for an army.'

They went home in a taxi, and Andrea was glad. Her feet were reminding her how much she'd used them that day.

'You go on up,' said Lex after he had opened the front door for her. 'I'm going to get some wine and fruit to go with the cheese. I'll be right back.'

Slowly she climbed the stairs. Oh, she was tired. She hadn't slept very much last night and she wasn't used to being on her feet as much as she'd been today. Once inside, she kicked off her shoes and plopped down on the couch. With a sigh she stretched out and closed her eyes. Ah, this was nice. Very comfy, this couch. She felt utterly happy and content. A perfect day it had been, all sunshine and no shadows.

When Lex came back she had almost drifted off to sleep, but not quite. Opening her eyes, she caught his glance.

'Don't bail out yet,' he said. 'The evening is

young.' He strode into the kitchen to dispose of his purchases, coming back only a minute later. He sat down on the edge of the couch.

'Tired?'

'Just pleasantly lazy.'

His dark eyes moved slowly over her face. 'You look happy,' he said then. 'And beautiful.'

Andrea grew warm under the look in his eyes and suddenly it seemed hard to breathe. Something thrilled between them and it became strangely quiet in the room. She lay very still, her heart beating in a wild, irregular rhythm, her eyes locked by his. She couldn't move, not for anything in the world. Lex was close, so very close, yet not touching, and all she wanted was for him to hold her, tell her he loved her. And the longing was like a pain that filled her body and there was nothing that could still that pain except the words she wanted to hear. But he was silent, so silent, with only his eyes looking at her, and she wanted to cry out, but her throat was locked and she could not speak.

She began to tremble, as if electrified by the tension stretching taut between them.

Then Lex stood up, very slowly, moving away from her. That strange look was back in his eyes, a pain, a fear she did not understand, and it frightened her more than anything—it froze something inside her. Please don't look at me like that! she cried silently. Oh, God, don't look at me like that! But she was too shaken to utter a sound and she watched him numbly as he moved around the partition.

She heard the opening of a cupboard, the gentle tinkling of glasses, and a few minutes later he appeared again carrying two glasses of wine.

His expression showed no emotion as he handed

her a glass. 'Try and see if you like this.'

She wanted to throw it in his face. Didn't he *know*? Didn't he *care*? How could he sit there and look at her, drinking wine as if nothing had happened? Well, she could do the same, couldn't she? What had she said this afternoon? 'I'm a quiet person.' It wouldn't help getting mad now. It wouldn't solve anything.

The glass trembled in her hand as she took a sip, then another. She didn't taste a thing. It could be anti-freeze for all she knew. 'I like it. What is it?'

Was there relief in his eyes? She wasn't sure.

'It's Moulin-à-Vent—should go well with the goat cheese we bought. With the Brie too.'

'I'll take your word for it.' She felt sick. A moment later the bell rang and she almost jumped.

Lex came to his feet. 'I'll get it.'

Through the open door she heard a voice calling from downstairs, but couldn't distinguish it. Lex poked his head back into the room.

'It's a man . . . I think.'

'You think?'

'It could be a scarecrow, or the Loch Ness monster. Shall I let him in?'

Andrea laughed despite herself. 'It's Pieter, and he's harmless.'

'That's a relief.'

By now Pieter had reached the top of the stairs, and Lex held open the door, waving him in. She had never seen him dressed in more bizarre fashion; he certainly had outdone himself.

The men introduced themselves gravely, but she saw the amusement glimmering in Lex's eyes. Pieter took off his hat and bowed with a flourish to Andrea.

'What do you think of my outfit?'

'Not much,' she said.

'The kids loved it,' he stated with satisfaction. 'I just came from the Children's Hospital.'

He accepted Lex's offer of wine and parked himself in a chair while Lex went to the kitchen.

'I won't stay long,' he said under his breath.

'I want you to stay. Please!'

He looked astounded. 'Until he leaves?'

That would take a while. 'No, just for an hour or so. Please!'

He did exactly that. He shared the cheese and bread and pâté with them, making himself quite at home. His company was like a balm, soothing Andrea's shaky emotions, calming her anger. His jokes relaxed the tension in the air. Evening was shadowing the room when finally he left and Andrea sat back with a sigh and slowly sipped the last of her wine. Taking a seat next to her, Lex stretched out his legs and made himself comfortable.

'Are all your friends like him?' he asked.

She saw the shine in his eyes and laughed. 'How many like him do you think there are?'

'Mmm . . . you've got a point there.' He paused, his expression puzzled. 'Somehow I never imagined you having a friend like him. You surprise me.'

She grinned. 'Good. I wouldn't want you to think I'm dull.'

'*Dull?* Good lord, never!'

She looked at him, but couldn't focus very well. She felt a little woozy. He didn't think she was dull. Well, that was one worry out of the way. She thought of Pieter and how often he had cheered her up when she'd hit rock bottom, and of the things he had told her about himself.

'Actually,' she began slowly, 'Pieter took me on as

a kind of project, a charity case.' She laughed at her own words.

There was a short silence. 'A project? A charity case? What the hell is that supposed to mean?'

'Well ... er. ...' Andrea laughed softly. 'Oh, never mind!' She put her head on his shoulder and sighed. 'I'm glad you're here.'

'So am I.'

'I talk too much when I've had a little to drink, you know that?'

'I do. I've noticed before.'

She smiled, rubbing her cheek against his shoulder. She felt happy and utterly content.

'You want coffee?' asked Lex after a silence.

'No, I just want to sit here with you. Don't leave.'

'All right, I won't.'

'I don't like it when you leave.'

'I'm not going to leave again, promise.'

She smiled again and closed her eyes.

'You're falling asleep,' he said, nudging her gently.

'No, I'm not, I'm just resting my eyes.'

'Oh, of course.'

She wasn't sleeping, just drifting along on a light cloud of euphoria.

'You know what I want?' she murmured.

'No.'

'I want you to kiss me.'

He kissed her, featherlike touches all over her face. His lips felt warm and soft.

'How's that?' he asked.

'Mmmm ... you must be the best kisser in the whole world.'

'I sure hope so.'

'Do you think I'm silly?'

'Do *you* think you're silly?'

She sighed. 'I don't know, but it sure feels good.'

He laughed.

She wanted to stay in his arms like this for ever. I'm not going to sleep, she told herself.

'You know what I want?' she said. 'You know what I really want?'

'Tell me.'

'I want you to make love to me. I want to make love to you.'

There was a terrible silence, an answer in itself.

Tears welled up in her eyes, rolling down her cheeks. 'Please, Lex, please. . . .'

'No, Andrea, no.' The words came out on a broken whisper. He lifted her into his arms, carried her into her room and carefully put her down on the bed.

She grasped his hand. 'Make love to me, please,' she whispered. 'Don't leave me. . . . You promised.'

His face was contorted. 'I'm not leaving.'

He began to ease off her clothes. With a sigh she closed her eyes.

She woke up in the middle of the night for no apparent reason. The next moment she realised she was wearing nothing but one lacy scrap of material and that she was alone in bed. With painful clarity memory rolled back.

'Oh, God!' she groaned, clenching her hands until the fingers dug into her palms. Lex was not here with her. She remembered what she had asked, remembered very well because she hadn't been drunk—not even close—just sleepy and a little groggy. She had asked and pleaded, and he had not stayed with her.

She pulled the nightshirt from under the pillow and slipped it on over her head. She needed to think, to get a clear picture of what was happening between Lex and herself.

Three glasses of wine didn't make her drunk—just a little silly and talkative ... and amorous in the right circumstances. Her head felt fine and the rest of her felt fine—the physical part of her at least.

Last night she had wanted Lex so much, so very much, and he had known. She had *begged* him to stay with her, but he had left, still he had left. He hadn't wanted to make love to her, he didn't want to make love to her at all—not last night, and not yesterday afternoon, and not the night before last. Something was wrong, terribly wrong, and nothing made sense. He loved her, everything he said and did pointed it out, she couldn't possibly be wrong about that. Why then. . . .

Anja.

It was as if her heart stopped at the very thought. Was Anja still there in his mind and thoughts, ruling his emotions? Could he never give himself completely to another woman because he had loved her too much for too long?

'Oh, God,' she moaned, 'please, please don't let it be true.' She pressed tight fists against her closed eyelids. She'd given him everything she had to give. Had it not been enough? Her stomach cramped—a hollow cramp of fear and pain.

So what now? What was she going to do about herself?

She straightened, as if in defence. I'm *not* going to compete with a dead wife! she thought hysterically. I want him to want *me*! Love *me*! And if he can't it's better he stay away from me! She pummelled the pillow, tears of furious frustration sliding down her cheeks.

She'd thought, hoped, prayed it was over now. That Lex was ready for a new beginning. She'd waited so long, so very long. And she couldn't wait any more. It was tormenting her, killing her.

Oh, she'd intended to be so good about all this. So accepting, so understanding, so rational. She understood, didn't she, how he had once loved another woman, as she had once loved another man. No jealousy, no wondering, no worrying.

Only it didn't work that way—after all was said and done she was nothing but a bundle of emotions and all the accepting and understanding flew right out of the window. She was hurting, and she couldn't go on this way.

I have to talk to him, she told herself. I'm going to tell him he can't do this to me.

At six o'clock she stumbled out of bed, dressed and made a pot of tea. She was drinking her third cup—drowning her nerves in tea—when Lex emerged from his room and went into the bathroom.

Andrea stood up, filled the kettle to heat water for a fresh pot of tea, and set the table for breakfast.

He wished her good morning, sat down and began to eat as if everything was normal. Andrea was tense with nerves, almost sick with the pain inside her. She couldn't eat, and she knew he was watching her and she couldn't bear it any longer. She pushed back her chair and stood up, her legs shaking. He rose to his feet as well, took a step towards her, reaching for her. She shrank away from him.

'Don't touch me,' she whispered. 'Please don't touch me.'

She saw the shock in his face and his hands

dropped by his sides. 'Andrea . . . what's wrong?'

'What's wrong? Oh, that's funny, that's really funny! That's what I was going to ask *you*! *You* tell *me*!'

He didn't answer. He just looked at her and from the expression in his eyes she knew that he was well aware of what she was talking about.

'I'm sorry,' he said at last, as if she'd accused him of something already. 'I'm sorry, Andrea.'

CHAPTER TEN

'TELL me why!' she burst out. 'Tell me *why* you're doing this to me! Last night . . . you made me *beg* you! I have never, *never* done that in my life!' She broke into tears. 'Oh, how could you! How could you do that to me!' She groped for the chair back in front of her, then felt herself propelled out of the kitchen and pushed down on the couch without ceremony.

'You were half asleep, for God's sake! You'd been on your feet practically all day and you'd been drinking! I put you to bed and you were asleep before I had your clothes off!'

'You . . . you could have stayed with me!' She was sobbing miserably. 'But . . . but you didn't want to, did you?'

'Andrea, listen to me.'

'No!' Shakily she came to her feet. 'You've been avoiding me. Don't you think I know? Something's wrong, and you're not telling me! I don't know what's going on, what it is you *want* from me!' Her voice had risen and she could no longer control the anger and the pain that had consumed her for the last few hours. 'I can't *take* this any more! I can't take you retreating from me all the time! It's Anja, isn't it? It's still her you really want!'

She saw Lex's face go white, but she couldn't help herself, couldn't stop the feeling of hysteria rising inside her. 'I'm right, aren't I? She's still there in everything you do and feel and want, isn't she? Well,

I'm not going to compete with that, I'm not even going to try!'

He lurched forward, took her arms in an iron grip and shook her. 'Stop it!' he ground out. 'Stop it now!'

Convulsive tremors shook her body. She braced her legs and clenched her hands, but tightening her muscles only seemed to make the shaking worse. She closed her eyes. 'Let me go,' she whispered. 'Please let me go.'

His hands relaxed and fell away from her arms. He stepped back, but only slightly. 'It has nothing to do with Anja,' he said huskily. 'Not in any way that you think. Please believe me.'

At this plea some of her usual calmness revived. She looked at him again and nodded slowly. 'I'm sorry, I. . . .' What was it she wanted to tell him? That she was scared of so many things—of losing him, of the memory of his wife whom he had loved so very much, scared of what was happening to them now, not understanding.

Andrea looked at him standing there—a man too big for the small confines of her attic, maybe too big for her life. She saw the contorted movements of his face, the taut muscles of his arms and legs as if he wanted to run, but couldn't. There was despair in his eyes and he looked like a lion caught in a trap, bereft of his freedom.

Freedom. Was he trapped here with her? Had she done that to him? Had her love ensnared him unwittingly so he had no way of getting out? It came to her then, in a moment of horrifying insight: he needed his freedom more than he needed her.

'Lex. . . .' His name was a whisper. She looked at

him, this man she loved more than she could ever tell him, and black panic surged up inside her. She sat down, bent her head and covered her face with her hands. There was only one thing to do and it was going to be more difficult than anything she'd ever done in her life.

'Yes?' His voice shook.

'Lex, I . . . I want you to leave.'

She wanted to die. Everything inside her cried out in revolt. No! No! No! The silence was suffocating, like heavy black smog. It's over, she thought, over, over, over. . . . She could never have loved again, never let herself become so vulnerable again. She had risked everything and lost it all.

She looked up, saw him staring at her in horrified disbelief, his face ashen.

'You don't mean that, Andrea.'

'Yes,' she whispered, not sure now she had the strength to go on. 'Yes, I mean it. I want you to go back to your daughter, make a new life, give her a home and settle down—all the things you want to do.' *All the things I wanted to be part of.*

It was incredible that she could look right into his eyes, tell him to leave her, not wavering, while inside she was dying.

His face was a mask of anguish. 'I don't understand,' he said unevenly. 'Why, Andrea, why?'

'Don't you know? Don't you see? Here with me you're trapped. You're not . . . not ready for . . . for another relationship. I don't want to keep you here if it's not right for you! Please. . . .' Her voice broke. She raised her hands in a feeble gesture of helplessness. 'I don't know what to do any more.' She wiped a hand across her face and felt the wetness of tears. 'I love you, Lex. I love you so very much, but it's not enough, is it?'

'You're wrong,' he said, 'you're so wrong.' He was
with her in seconds, pulling her up against him. 'I
love you too,' he groaned. 'Oh, God, I love you too,
and I'm not leaving, not ever.' It seemed as if the
words were wrenched from him and the next
moment he was kissing her, but there was nothing
gentle or tender about it. It was a violent struggle—
not with her, but with himself, with his emotions.
He was fighting something and she knew not what.
He had never kissed her like this before—there was
despair and fear and hunger all mixed up, she could
feel it, sense it. He didn't stop, kept going on and on
and on, crushing her against him with a wild man's
strength.

Andrea pushed against his chest, tears of pain
stinging her eyes. 'You're hurting me! Lex, please!
You're *hurting* me!'

He let go of her instantly, looking down at her
with eyes wide with shock. 'I'm sorry,' he groaned.
'I'm sorry.' He took a deep breath, raking his fingers
through his hair. He looked like a man going through
a living nightmare.

'It doesn't matter,' she said tonelessly. His wild
outburst had shaken her. She did not understand
him any more, she didn't understand anything.

Lex dropped his weight heavily on to the couch,
pulling her down next to him. He was trembling, as
she was trembling herself, and she thought of that
other time, a long time ago, when she had held him
in her arms, when he had finally given way to the
grief that had been tormenting him. Only this time
she did not know what was wrong. She watched him
as he lay back against the cushions, his eyes closed,
fear inside her like a living thing.

'Lex,' she whispered, 'what's wrong?'

He bent forward, elbows on his knees, and covered his face with his hands. 'I'm an idiot,' he said huskily, 'an irrational, illogical idiot.'

She touched his shoulder. 'Why? What are you afraid of? Tell me, please tell me.'

He raised his head slowly and his eyes looked directly into hers. 'I'm afraid of losing you. I'm afraid something might happen to you too.'

It took a moment, a fraction of a moment for his words to sink in. It was clear to her then, clear like neon lights flashing in the dark. *'What you don't have, you can't lose.'* Those were her own words, spoken more than a year ago.

'Oh, Lex . . . I . . . .' Her voice broke. 'Lex, I can't . . . I can't promise you not to die.'

His arms came around her, as if in comfort to her. 'I know, I know.'

She leaned against him, impatiently wiping away tears, wishing there was something she could tell him, something that would help, but there was nothing. The minutes passed in silence.

Early Sunday morning. Everything was so quiet—people still sleeping, virtually no traffic disturbing the peace. Sunlight sneaked through the slanted window, dropping a patch of light on to the half-finished bedspread folded up on the floor. Sunday morning. In a couple of hours church bells would ring all over the city calling people to worship. Not a time for crisis and confrontation, this.

After a long time Lex stirred. 'Andrea,' he said softly, 'I've loved you for a long time; you know that, don't you?'

She nodded. 'I thought you did.'

'I nearly told you so in January, only . . . I wasn't

so sure it was for all the right reasons. Our relationship wasn't what you'd call an ordinary one. So
I said nothing, and I went back to Bolivia.' His voice
was very steady now. 'I tried to socialise, go to
parties in La Paz, go out with other women.' He
paused and looked at her. 'It didn't work. I couldn't
get interested, not even physically. I kept thinking
about you. All the time, I could only think of you.
And then I came back. You opened the door and
from that first moment I saw you, saw your face and
your eyes, I knew that you were the one I wanted,
that I loved you for all the right reasons.' She felt
the slight tensing of his arm around her. 'And then,
Andrea, it hit me and I panicked. I thought, oh,
God, I can't do this ... I couldn't go through it
again. What if ... what if. ... She could be dead
tomorrow, hit by a car, or God knows what, and I'll
die too.'

She could feel a tremor go through him and she
saw his eyes, deep pools of emotion, and she shivered.
She didn't trust herself to speak.

Lex took a steadying breath. 'I was too much of a
coward to face up to the risks of life, to say right out
in the open that I loved you and accept the consequences. Every time I held you in my arms, wanting
you, wanting you so badly, I panicked. I was
terrified of getting hurt again.'

She swallowed at the lump in her throat. 'I wish
I'd known ... I wish I'd known.'

'I'm sorry I hurt you. I didn't mean to.' He lifted
her chin. 'Andrea, are you worried about my
memories of Anja?'

She swallowed. 'I suppose so,' she said miserably.
'Last night when I woke up and ... and you weren't
with me, I thought ... I kept thinking that ... that

every time you came near me you realised it was. . . .'
Oh, why couldn't she talk? Why was she crying
again?

'. . . it was Anja I wanted, not you?'

'Yes. Oh, I'm sorry, I'm sorry. I don't even
understand myself any more. But you were acting so
strangely, and I'd worried about it before because
. . . because she seemed so different from me.'

He wiped the tears from her face. 'Yes,' he said,
his tone quiet and steady. 'She had a different personality. You're not like her—I wouldn't even want
you to be. You're not a replacement, not a substitute.
You are you and I love you for what you are. I love
you in a different way, too. Not more, not less, just
differently.' His face was very calm now, his eyes
clear as they looked right at her, his expression one
of quiet strength. 'I don't think any two love rela-
tionships are ever the same.' Pausing a moment, he
smiled. 'And don't tell me I'm anything like that
fire-fighting hero you were married to before!'

She laughed a little shakily. 'Oh, no! You're right,
I know. I just got so emotional about it, I was afraid
of what was going on. I didn't understand. And I
was thinking too, that maybe I was part of the problem somehow, that you might be better off without
me. You said it had nothing to do with Anja, so
then it had to be me.'

'So you told me to leave.' His voice sounded
strange. 'Still thinking about me first, weren't you?'

'I love you,' she said.

Lex gathered her up against him. 'Yes, I don't
have a sliver of a doubt about that.' He kissed her
gently. 'And now you know it wasn't Anja, it wasn't
you—it was *me*. I'll get over these feelings—I expect
they're normal enough under the circumstances.

And besides, I have no choice. I'm not leaving you again. I'm not going anywhere without you.' He stood up, pulling her to her feet and into his arms. He kissed her, a long, wonderfully exciting kiss that left her breathless.

'I love you,' he murmured, repeating the words over and over again as if making up for lost time. 'I love you, I love you, I love you.' He let out a deep sigh. 'Do you have any idea how good it feels to tell you that?' He kissed her again, not waiting for a reply. 'I'm going to make love to you,' he whispered against her lips, 'and nothing and nobody is going to stop me.' He drew himself away slightly so he could look into her eyes. 'Andrea, I want you so much . . . so much . . . it's been hell these last couple of nights. I don't know why . . . how. . . .' He closed his eyes and drew her close again. She could feel the hard thud of his heart . . . or was it her own?

'Come on,' he whispered, swinging her up into his arms, and carrying her from the room.

They stood together near the bed, close together, eyes locked. Lex had never looked at her this way before and a wave of emotion washed over her. He was hers to love, this man, hers to make happy. She was trembling, waiting, feeling the intangible current flowing between them as the silence stretched. His hands reached out, taking both of hers in his.

'Andrea,' he said huskily, 'here we are, you and I, just you and I. There is nothing standing between us now, no secrets, no unspoken doubts. Right?'

She nodded silently.

'Nothing,' he repeated as he slowly began to remove their clothing, holding her eyes all the time.

Andrea closed her eyes, feeling his hands touching her, his mouth caressing her face. She clung closer to him, impatient, searching for his mouth, joining in his kiss in a mutual rapturous delight.

They moved towards the bed, not letting go of each other, lying down together, arms and legs entwined.

His hands were doing wonderful things to her, setting her all aglow, making her heart go faster and faster, taking her higher and higher in a sphere where no time or place existed.

There would never be enough words, never the right ones to tell him of the depth of her love. But this was better, so much better. . . . Her hands, her mouth, her body needed no words. She wanted to make him happy, she wanted so much to make him happy again. Now, after all the waiting and all the uncertainties, the time had come and she knew what to do. She could feel him trembling against her and he opened his eyes and looked at her, dazed. 'My God,' he muttered, 'do you know what you're doing to me?'

'Are you complaining?' she whispered, and he groaned, kissing her fiercely in response. She had longed for this, all those long, lonely months. Longed for his body close against hers, longed for him to make her feel alive again. There was no reserve in him now, no pulling back—it was much too late for that now.

She lay in his embrace, not stirring, not talking. She felt overwhelmed by the sheer wonder of his loving—perfect, beautiful, complete. He felt warm against her, his body curved around hers, every inch of him touching her. She could feel the power of him, the strength of him even as he lay still against her. She could sense the peace in him too, the same peace

that permeated every part of her. Everything was
right—wonderfully, beautifully right.

A deep, contented sigh came unbidden. At the
sound of it he opened his eyes and gave her a slow
smile. 'Happy?'

She buried her face in his neck, and sighed again.
'Yes. Hopelessly, helplessly and deliriously.'

He laughed. 'Keep it up!'

Andrea lifted her face to look at him. 'I intend to.
Did I tell you I have three weeks of vacation
coming?' she whispered.

'You did. Let's go to the beach.' He was whispering too, as if they were concocting a conspiracy. 'My
oldest sister and her husband own a summer cottage
near Bergen aan Zee. We can have it for a couple of
weeks.'

She eyed him suspiciously. 'How do you know?'

Lex grinned smugly. 'I checked with them last
week, just in case I'd manage to find some luscious
female who'd like to spend some time with me.'

She grinned. 'I'm flattered you think I'm luscious.
When can we go? Today?'

They lay in the dunes, protected from the wind,
wearing jeans and sweaters. The sun was shining,
but the coolness of fall already tingled in the air.

'What do you think?' asked Lex.

'About what?'

'About us. You and me and the sun and the sand
and the sky.'

'Everything.'

'Good, very good,' he murmured, trailing a lazy
finger down her nose and lips. 'How do you feel?'

'Very whole . . . very complete.'

'Mmm, me too. What are we going to do about it?'

'About what?'

'About us,' he said.

'Everything.'

'Sounds good to me.' He began to kiss her, his hands sliding under her sweater.

'Not here!' She laughed and twisted away from him, but he pinned her under him in the sand and there was no way to escape.

'Don't run away from me,' he ordered.

'I'll try my very best,' she returned meekly, closing her eyes against the bright sky.

'I want to ask you something.'

'Go ahead.'

'Why don't we get married?'

Elation like glorious sunshine filled her. She had not worried about it for a moment—they'd get married when the time was right, she'd never doubted that—still, his question was like an exquisite gift, a shining jewel, this offering of his commitment to their love.

She half-opened her eyes, pretending drowsiness. 'Mmm . . . what?'

'You heard me. Let's get married.'

'Mmm . . . I don't know. I don't think we know each other very well.' Through her lashes she watched his face, the momentary incredulity, then saw the laughter going all through him until she couldn't contain her own. His hold on her had slackened and she slid away from him. She wanted to run, dance, shout for joy. She made a dash for it, slipped in the dry sand, scrambled up again and ran. He raced after her, slipped and caught her by the ankle, dragging her down into the sand with him.

'I asked you to marry me,' he growled, 'and you didn't answer me.'

Andrea wriggled helplessly against him. 'I have to think about it.'

'No. You'll have to decide right now—there's a line waiting.'

Laughter filled her, flowed over until he silenced her with his mouth. It was a short, impatient kiss, and when he looked up again the laughter had gone from his face. His eyes were dark and intense.

'*Ja of nee?*' he asked on a low note. 'Tell me yes or no.'

'Yes.' She pulled his face down and kissed him deeply. 'Yes, yes, yes. And you didn't have to ask, you already knew.'

'I wanted to hear you say it.'

There was a dark glow deep in his eyes and a delicious little tremor ran all the way through her. 'I'll say it again,' she whispered. 'I want us to be married and make a new life together. I'm going to make you happy, very, very happy.' She was still whispering, as if she were divulging some deep dark secret. She looked down for a moment, then back at his face. 'I'll do all I can to be a good mother to Martha . . . if . . . if she'll have me.' She swallowed, then, saw the stillness in his face, the intense awareness in his eyes. 'I want you to come home to me every night,' she went on, 'and tell me about your day—the good things, and the bad things too. I want us to sleep together in a big bed with my orange bedspread on it and I want to wake up every morning with you in my arms.' She smiled into his eyes. 'That's all I want,' she said lightly. 'Nothing special, just the ordinary stuff.'

Lex groaned and closed his eyes. 'Yeah, just the ordinary stuff. I'll never take it for granted, I swear.' He kissed her drunkenly, but after a few moments he stopped abruptly, rolled off her and flung himself on his stomach in the sand, resting his face on his arms.

Laughing, she stroked his neck. 'What's wrong?'

'Nothing's *wrong*,' he muttered. 'And don't act so damned innocent. Do you want to get ravished right here in the dunes?'

'Now that I think about it, it seems kind of romantic.'

Lex groaned and lifted his face, giving her a tormented look. 'Stop it! I'm suffering enough as it is.' He shrugged off her teasing hand and dropped his head back on his arms.

Grinning, Andrea lay back and squinted up at the blue sky where bright clouds drifted along on a steady breeze. Seagulls swept overhead, and in the distance she could hear the waves breaking on to the beach. Contentedly she stretched and took a deep breath, smelling the salty tang of sea air.

She stole a glance at Lex next to her, seeing his whole length draped in the sand looking quite relaxed now. There was sand all over him, his hair included. Was he sleeping? She sighed and closed her eyes. It was quiet for quite some time.

'Do you realise,' she asked after a while, 'that, except for Sylvia, I haven't met a single member of your family? Not even your daughter?'

'Don't worry, you will.'

'What if she doesn't like me?'

He turned around on his back and grinned. 'Martha will love you. And you'll love her.'

'Who says?'

'*I* say. She's smart, receptive, sensitive. . . .'

'Oh, Lex, be serious!' She sat up.

'I *am* serious.' He sat up too, and he was no longer

grinning. 'Are you worried about it?'

'Of course I am! I mean, I *think* about it.'

'Well, I think about it too,' he said soberly. 'As a matter of fact I've thought about it before now, and I've talked to Martha, started to prepare her.'

'You have? When?'

'This summer when she was with me in Bolivia. I talked to her about marriage in general terms. I didn't tell her about you because I had no certainty, but I explained to her that it would be so very nice to be a whole family again. That I would like to have a wife, and that it would be good for her to have a new mother.'

Andrea was silent. She scooped up handfuls of sand and slowly let it trickle through her fingers. Martha. She remembered the bright eyes and the unruly curls of the girl on the picture, remembered the clear voice on the tape. Would Martha want her for a new mother?

'Lex?' She looked up to meet his eyes. 'Could we have Martha here for a couple of days next week? Before I meet anyone else of your family? Could we be together for a while, just the three of us?' She went still as she saw the expression on his face.

'Just the three of us,' he repeated softly. He closed his eyes and drew her against him. 'You really want her, don't you?' he asked unevenly.

She put her arms around him, feeling the sand on his back, gritty and scratchy. Inside she felt velvety soft.

'If she's yours, she's mine.'

He tightened his embrace. 'I love you . . . oh, I love you.'

They were silent for a while.

'There's something I want you to know,' Andrea

said at last. 'When . . . whenever Martha wants to know about . . . about her mother, about . . . Anja, I want you to feel safe talking about her in front of me.'

Lex drew away slowly and looked at her, his eyes full of infinite love. His hands reached up and smoothed her hair away from her face.

'Andrea . . .' His voice shook. 'Andrea, I wish I knew what to say.'

Somewhere in the cottage he unearthed a kite, a huge contraption of orange and blue and green. He was jubilant about his find, and Andrea laughed when he insisted on going to the beach at once to try it out. She sat in the sand, arms around her knees, watching him as he made the dragon-kite soar through the air in all its glory of colour. Pulling and relaxing the string, he made it do the most intricate movements, laughing and shouting with enthusiasm as the dragon dipped and dived, soared up and floated around.

He stood out against the wide expanse of sky, tall and dark and straight. Andrea tucked a strand of windblown hair behind her ear and swallowed. He was like an exuberant kid without a worry in the world, the kite in all its free flying splendour and expression of his joy. He didn't seem to get enough of it, as if all this was some old primitive ritual to chase away bad spirits and attract the good.

She had never seen him so exultant, so radiant. He looked years younger, a life removed from the silent stranger she had once found in her attic—a long, long time ago.

Exhausted at last, he plopped himself down next to her in the sand and began to fold up the kite. His hair had fallen over his forehead. His eyes were bright and he looked at her with a smile that lit up his whole face.

'How did I do?'

'You were fantastic. You *are* fantastic.'

He grinned wolfishly. 'Yeah, I know.' He put down the kite and raked his hair back with both hands. He reached for her, his face suddenly serious, and wrapped his arms around her and held her close. 'I didn't know,' he said unevenly, 'that I could ever feel this way again. That I could ever feel so utterly happy again.'

Andrea rubbed her cheek against his, not answering.

'You know,' he said after a pause. 'We'll get old together, you and I. I know it, I feel it. Nothing is going to happen to you, and nothing is going to happen to me. We'll grow old together, *ancient*.' He spoke with great conviction as if he'd made a contract with fate that could never be broken.

She raised her face to look at him. 'Yes,' she said quietly, smiling, 'I know. I feel it too.'

Harlequin® Plus

A WORD ABOUT THE AUTHOR

Karen van der Zee is an author on the move. She was born in Holland, studied in the United States and then married a man whose work, as an agricultural adviser in developing countries, has taken the family to such faraway places as Liberia and Ghana.

It was in Ghana, in fact, that Karen stumbled across a Harlequin Romance for the first time—at a neighbor's home. Karen, who already had poetry and short stories published in Dutch, was now fluent in English. After reading her first Harlequin, she knew she wanted to expand into this field of writing.

The result of that desire was *Sweet Not Always* (Romance #2334), her first novel, set in the primitive jungle of Ghana.

Karen enjoys the opportunity of being able to introduce her readers to new places and cultures, and she would like to get to know her audience more personally. "You can say you write for yourself," she explains, "but that's not really true."

Karen, her husband, Gary, and their family make their permanent home in the United States. For most women a move to another country—or another continent—means pulling up roots. For Karen van der Zee it means a chance to discover a brand-new setting for a brand-new book.

Legacy of
PASSION
BY CATHERINE KAY

A love story begun long ago comes full circle...

Venice, 1819: Contessa Allegra di Rienzi, young, innocent, unhappily married. She gave her love to Lord Byron—scandalous, irresistible English poet. Their brief, tempestuous affair left her with a shattered heart, a few poignant mementos—and a daughter he never knew about.

Boston, today: Allegra Brent, modern, independent, restless. She learned the secret of her great-great-great-grandmother and journeyed to Venice to find the di Rienzi heirs. There she met the handsome, cynical, blood-stirring Conte Renaldo di Rienzi, and like her ancestor before her, recklessly, hopelessly lost her heart.